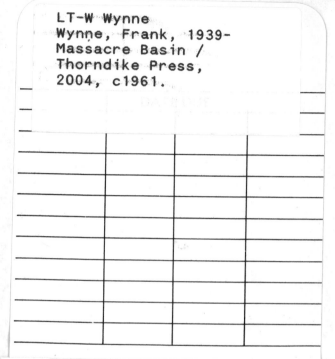

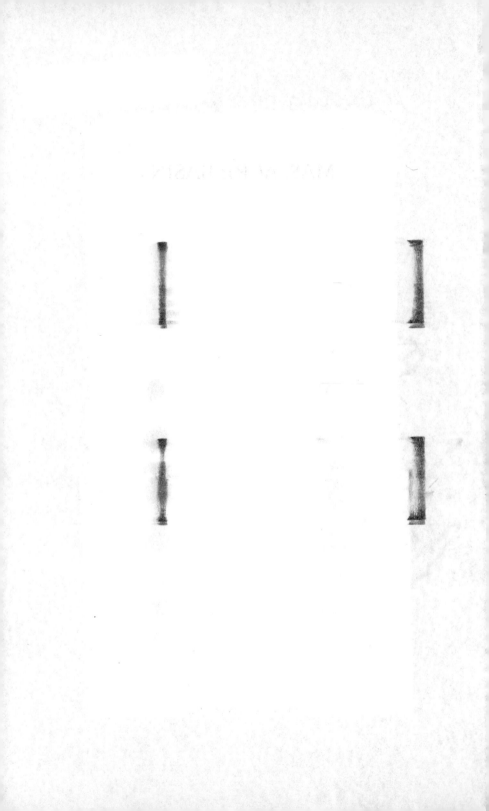

# MASSACRE BASIN

Frank Wynne

**CHIVERS**

**THORNDIKE**

This Large Print book is published by BBC Audiobooks Ltd, Bath, England and by Thorndike Press®, Waterville, Maine, USA.

Published in 2004 in the U.K. by arrangement with Frank Wynne.

Published in 2004 in the U.S. by arrangement with Golden West Literary Agency.

U.K. Hardcover   ISBN 1–4056–3071–X (Chivers Large Print)
U.K. Softcover   ISBN 1–4056–3072–8 (Camden Large Print)
U.S. Softcover   ISBN 0–7862–6830–1 (Nightingale)

The text of this Large Print edition is unabridged.
Other aspects of the book may vary from the original edition.

Set in 16 pt. New Times Roman.

Printed in Great Britain on acid-free paper.

**British Library Cataloguing in Publication Data available**

**Library of Congress Control Number: 2004107029**

LT–W

# CHAPTER ONE

Cold reached through the blankets, through his clothes, through his skin; a biting cold with strong jaws and knife-pointed teeth. It scraped his bones and chewed harshly at his bowels while he felt the prickly surface of his flesh and the uncontrollable tremor of all his muscles. By his two-dollar watch it was noon, but by the sky it might have been midnight.

The line cabin's chinked log walls trembled and rattled and, around the door and windows where the chinking had chipped away, a fifty-mile wind galloped through, shrieking the screams of a mustang with a lion on its back. A sheet of old newspaper he had used to hold bacon was flapping around the room, a strange and ragged white bird.

The norther had come whistling down out of the Grand Canyon country. Marching on rushing black clouds, driving the temperatures down fifty degrees and herding every living thing to shelter. Clay Sebastian, thirty-one years old in this spring of the great blizzard, had never in his third-of-a-century of existence experienced a storm of such violence on the range. He had pushed longhorn cattle all the way up from Texas through Kansas and Colorado to Williams County, Wyoming, and had wintered twice in the north. But those

1

winters couldn't hold a candle to this springtime Arizona norther.

Just now he had fifteen years as a cattleman behind him—some as chore boy, some as cowhand, and most recently, three seasons as foreman of Hat. The result, he observed with a dry scowl, was eight dollars in the pockets of his denims, his own cavvy of five horses, and as much cow savvy as many a man had taken a lifetime to learn. He also, at the moment, owned three blankets, a sheepskin mackinaw, long-handled underwear, two pairs of wool socks, a pair of Justin boots, two flannel shirts and a Stetson hat—all of which he was wearing as he huddled on the bunk in the line shack and heard the roar of the storm highballing southward.

'I ought to be out there saving those cows,' he had told himself a while ago. But he had realized quickly that going out in the white hell would accomplish nothing. A lucky man would find a dead steer, slit the belly and crawl inside the carcass for warmth until the storm went on. An unlucky man would perish.

Out on the land, life was draining off the prairie. The length of Massacre Basin was swept clean by the blizzard. Deer and antelope and coyotes were later to be found frozen where the storm had caught them. Cattle ran in panicked hordes before the forty-below winds. Flying ice and debris and branches were carried along in the backwash of the gale.

Some cattle, after the storm, would be found three hundred miles from their home ranges.

And if they get found by somebody like Lew Kohlmeier, Clay thought, like as not they'll never be returned to their rightful owners. An ill wind blew nobody good; Kohlmeier's crew of rustlers would find the storm's aftermath good pickings.

True, a few strays would come drifting in from time to time, from the higher sheltered gulches in the Monarchs, from neighboring ranges, from isolated safety areas like Aztec Canyon and Peacock Gap. But of the herd of upwards of twenty thousand head, Clay Sebastian wondered how many would remain to Hat.

He crawled out of his blankets and put more wood on the fire he had kept roaring in the cabin's pot-bellied stove. Then, with energy born of need, he hauled the heavy double-deck bunk closer to the stove and lay back, not more than a yard from the fire. But he still felt the searing cold of the howling, mysterious day. He had no fat on his bones to insulate him.

Some wind-driven object, a log or animal, smashed against the outside wall, shaking the shack. That single report, startling against the constant roar all around, woke him from a half-stupor. He looked at his watch: three o'clock. The fire needed more wood. He tore shelves off the walls, broke them over his knee and built up the fire; and then walked around the room, stamping his feet, beating his arms against his sides to thaw the blood and boost his sluggish circulation. Seeps of wind that found passage through cracks in the walls set up a whirling current in the room; when he built a cigarette and tried to light it, three matches fluttered out before he managed to fire the tobacco. As he sucked on the warm smoke, he suddenly realized he hadn't eaten all day.

There was still a chunk from the bacon slab. He sliced it, whipped together some sourdough biscuits and boiled a gallon of coffee. The bacon burned black, but he ate it. The biscuits came out two textures harder than Colorado granite, so he gave that up and pitched them into the fire. For the rest of the afternoon, and half through the night, he kept replenishing the coffeepot and downing the brew.

Some time during the raging hours after midnight he fell asleep in the blankets, having just refilled the stove with broken spars from the top bunk.

When he next looked at his watch it was close to five in the morning. Something had awakened him and for a brief while he lay still, trying to discover what it had been. Then he knew what had roused him. The storm had not stopped, but the norther had died down. In place of a roar there was a whistle and the steady patter of rain on the roof. He went to the window.

It was light hail. But he could feel a touch of warmth in the air. He could tell that the temperature had risen markedly overnight. The barn was in plain sight where it had been invisible yesterday. Up above the solid mass of cloud was distantly gray instead of solid black. The norther, horrible in its rage, had moved on.

Sebastian grinned. He ran a coarse-knuckled hand through his brick-red hair and spoke aloud. 'Well, old wind, I've played the game by your rules and won. Nobody beats me in a tough game.'

He scorched the rest of the bacon on the stove, mixed another unsuccessful batch of sourdoughs, cursed, and set the coffeepot on to boil.

When he finished his meal he buckled his mackinaw, turned up the collar, and stepped outside the door for the first time in forty hours, to test the air. It was six miles from here, the Rifle Springs boundary cabin, to Peyote Wells at the far end of the Flats. Then, from Nine-Mile Flats to Hat headquarters on Parrott Creek was another nine miles. The snow on the ground reached above his knees. Fifteen miles of bucking that would be tough. But it would be tougher after nightfall. He decided to leave now.

He rolled his blankets and extinguished the

fire, and plowed through the yard to the barn. He found with some relief that his pinto had weathered the norther in good health. Its shaggy coat, with the added abundant thickness of hay, had protected it. He fed it a sackful of oats, gave it a rub-down, and cinched up.

Mounted, he ducked his head to clear the door, and rode out onto the land, a tall man on horseback bucking the deep drifts. In the saddle his shape loomed deceptively bulky, bundled in his many layers of clothing. Long legs and flat hips supported a tall back and wide, pointed shoulders. His neck was strangely thick and his jaw was a long, clean shelf above it; his nose was thin and straight; high cheek-bones thrust out against sun-darkened flesh; and gray eyes were overhung by bushy red brows. A casual survey of his face in repose might suggest that this was a man of solid ambition, a man who liked a good fight and was accustomed to winning, a man who knew his trade, and a man who, by his eyes, watched the world with an unusual combination of keen perceptiveness and latent humor.

He dropped the pinto through the shallow canyon above Peyote Wells, crossed the swollen stream and mounted the opposite bank, and turned more directly north toward Hat headquarters. His chosen path lifted him higher on the central plateau of Massacre

Basin, humped over two or three long flat ridges, and finally, near sundown, led into the vast, sprawling center of activity of Hat.

This was the headquarters of Jesse Parrott's cattle empire. From here, Parrott's Hat stretched in all directions across the leagues of snow-covered range. Its nearest boundary to the west was eleven miles from his yard. To the north it stretched fifteen miles past Dragoon Springs almost to the looping bend of the Massacre River. To the east its boundary lines, vaguely defined, followed the irregular protrusions of the lower slopes of the Monarchs. To the south, it stretched clear across Nine-Mile Flats to the cabin at Rifle Springs where Sebastian had spent the last two days. Four hundred thousand acres were Hat; acres that had, until two days ago, been populated by Jesse Parrott, his family, his foreman Clay Sebastian, and his picked crew of eighteen sun-blackened riders, and twenty thousand head of mixed stock, some of it blooded and some of it descended directly from Parrott's original herd of Texas longhorns.

During the whole of his nine-hour ride, Sebastian had seen no live cattle, and only a few scattered dead ones, and the single gathering of a few hundred frozen, trampled carcasses at the base of the wall at Peyote Wells. The bulk of the herd, he guessed, had been driven south into the rough country of the Breaks, barren unclaimed badlands below Rifle Springs. As foreman of Hat, the herd was his responsibility; and anxiety over the wholesale destruction wrought by the storm settled heavily on his shoulders.

He unsaddled the pony and once again curried it and left the main barn to walk the length of the *remuda* corral's fence. A scatter of lesser outbuildings converged on the center of the yard where the long adobe bunkhouse, on one side, and the cavvy corral and tack barn on the other, formed the shoulders of a wide path leading to the boarded veranda of the sprawling main house.

This was Jesse Parrott's palace, a huge building, half log and half adobe, built strong to withstand Apache raiders, and constructed more for utility than for beauty. A dozen thick, tall cottonwoods surrounded the house, and behind it a curling row of sycamores, cottonwoods and lesser mesquites holding pens, horse and cattle corrals, and branding chutes stretched west from here a distance of almost half a mile. Sebastian paused. Not a living thing stirred. He guessed that most of the surviving horses had been driven inside the four huge barns for protection.

Smoke issued from the cookhouse chimney, the bunkhouse, and four different chimneys of the main house. Clay mounted the five steps to the veranda, and knocked at the great oak door.

It was not Jesse Parrott who admitted him, but Ray Queene, and this surprised Sebastian. Queene showed no spark of pleasure when he greeted Sebastian. 'Where in hell you been, Clay?'

'Rifle Springs.' From habit he removed his black hat when he stepped inside.

No one else occupied the huge parlor. Above the massive fireplace, Jesse Parrott's portrait, commissioned on his last trip to Chicago, hung in somber stillness; it was the image of a man as tall as the times in which he lived.

Sebastian said, 'Where's Jesse?'

Ray Queene touched his arm. Queene's dark, secretive eyes were dull. 'Hold it a minute, Clay. I've got bad news.'

Sebastian met his even glance. 'Spit it out.'

'Jesse and Molly got caught in the storm, halfway out from Arrowhead. The gale turned their buckboard over.'

Breath whistled out of Sebastian as though a blow had struck his stomach. 'What happened, Ray?'

'They started walking,' Queene said, in a very tired tone. 'Mrs. Parrott passed out after a while and Jesse picked her up and carried her. Six miles, he carried her, Clay! But it was too late when he got here. She's dead.'

Sebastian's head was down; his eyes were looking at the floor but he wasn't seeing it. 'And Jesse?'

'In bed,' Queene said quietly. 'He's got a fever. I don't know how bad it is. I sent Lucio into Arrowhead for the doc this morning. They ought to get here tonight.'

Sebastian strode half the length of the room, unbuckled his heavy gunbelt with its holstered revolver, and hung it over the back of a chair. 'Is he awake?'

'He was a few minutes ago,' Queene said.

'I'll go in.'

'He's taking it pretty hard,' Queene warned. 'About his wife.'

Almost through the door, Sebastian turned and halted. 'How about Nora?'

'She's all right,' Queene drawled. 'Stayed here all through it. But she's worried about her old man. She's in with him now.'

Sebastian nodded and swung into the hallway. He walked straight through to the thickly paneled door at its far end, and knocked. The door opened and Nora Parrott looked up at him. He saw mixed fright and concern in her glance.

Sebastian said, 'Can I come in?'

'He's—' she started.

Her answer was cut off by a bull-throated roar from the room behind her, 'Is that Clay? Well, send him in here, Nora. Don't stand there and jaw all night.'

Nora stepped aside and Sebastian entered the room.

It was a massive room. Mahogany paneling

10

covered the high walls and in the center of Sebastian's attention stood the four-posted cherrywood bed Jesse had had shipped all the way from Boston.

He had never seen Jesse Parrott look so small. In a flannel nightshirt and bundled under heaps of blankets, his flesh still looked cold despite the great fire roaring in the big fireplace. Its flicker irregularly illuminated the man's leathery features. His big jaw and wide cheeks seemed gaunted; his flesh was pallid and Sebastian felt the tremor of his thick hand when he took it. Sebastian said, 'I guess you know how I feel about Molly, Jesse.'

'My faith is gone,' Parrott said. Sebastian couldn't help hearing the quiver of his deep voice. 'There was no reason for this, Clay.'

'The Lord moves in strange ways, Jesse.'

'No call to do this to her,' Jesse said. His bull head, gray and lined with wrinkles, shook back and forth. 'How was it down at Rifle Springs?'

'Rough,' Sebastian said. He rolled a cigarette and handed it to the old man, and held the candle flame to it. 'The only cows I saw today were dead.'

'They're all driven south,' Jesse said, in a tone that carried no interest whatever. 'We'll have to comb the breaks.'

Sebastian nodded and lit his own cigarette. Jesse was still talking, probably to keep his mind off his own tragedy. 'Chances are Lew

Kohlmeier's down there already with as big a crew as he could lay hands on. When you take the outfit down after those cows, boy, you may have to fight Kohlmeier.'

'I drove him off Hat once before,' Sebastian said. 'I'll do it again if I have to. Lew's skin's worth more to him than any bunch of Hat cattle.'

'Don't underestimate that long-looper, Clay. He's sly and he's tough. I've been at a stalemate with him for five years, ever since he moved himself into the Monarchs and took over Peacock Gap. You watch him.'

'Sure,' Sebastian said softly. The light behind Jesse's eyes was very dim. His breathing was labored and there were beads of sweat on his forehead.

Jesse said suddenly, 'I'm not going to make it, Clay.'

'You're crazy,' Sebastian said quickly, feeling the shock of Jesse's statement.

Nora Parrott, who had remained by the door all this time, came quickly across the room to rest her hand on her father's arm. 'Don't talk that way, Jesse. You'll be all right. You'll be in the saddle again in another week.'

'Not this time,' Jesse said. His voice sounded hoarse. 'This time your mother's gone.'

Nora's pretty, dark head dropped. 'I know. But you mustn't give up the fight because of that.'

12

'Maybe,' he said, 'maybe I want to be with her.' His hand reached up to grasp Sebastian's sleeve and his husky tone became urgent. 'Clay, I want you to run Hat for us. Hat needs you now. You're the only man in Massacre Basin that can hold it together. When I'm gone the wolves will come out of their black holes and gang up on Hat. They'll be like a pack after a crippled antelope. I want your word you'll stick.'

'I'll stick, Jesse,' Sebastian said quietly. 'You have my word. But you're staying too.'

'Your word,' the old man muttered. 'Ah, that's good.' His eyes were focused aimlessly in the air. 'I want to rest.'

'Sure, Jesse.' Sebastian met Nora's glance, nodded, and walked out of the room.

## CHAPTER TWO

'I got in it myself,' Ray Queene said. His blond head dipped when he picked a brand out of the fireplace's great maw to light his cigarette. 'Latigo and I were comin' back from Dragoon Springs. Took us near four hours to make the last two miles, after the wind started blowing and the sky caved in. Damn, I wish Lucio'd get here with the doctor.'

Queene stood spread-legged by the fire, gazing into it. Now he whirled away and

13

tramped across the room to post himself before a front window.

The silence advanced until Sebastian heard a weak cough scratch through the door. On that signal he moved to join Queene at the window. Feeling useless and hating the feeling, Sebastian turned back to the huge, somber oil portrait over the fireplace. The Jesse he had seen a few moments ago in the great bedroom was only a pale shadow of the Jesse in the painting, a big-shouldered, spade-jawed man who had been tough and tenacious enough to drive a herd of Texas longhorns the fifteen hundred miles from Matagorda, Texas, through Comanche country, through the deserts of New Mexico, through the barren and hostile Apache territory of Arizona to Massacre Basin. Here, with water, hundreds of square miles of good bunch grass, and the natural boundaries formed by the Massacre River, the rugged peaks of the Monarchs, and the impassable badlands of the Breaks, he had founded his empire and peopled it with cattle. Every year since then had seen a cattle drive, each one successively larger, from Hat headquarters to the railroad's shipping pens at Benson. Every year had seen at least one incident in which the Hat cowboys pitted themselves against the hard-case moonlight riders of Lew Kohlmeier. Every year had seen men and cattle die, of disease and bad water and Indian attack and exposure to stinging

14

blizzard and scorching drought. And as the years had passed they had witnessed the growing power of Hat and the lesser satellite ranches that began to surround it. To the north and west, Buck DeSpain's Pitchfork; to the west, Rob MacKenzie's Pennant; to the south and west, and second in size only to Hat, Fletch Diedrich's Slash-D, a big ranch moved bodily from the crowding plains of central Texas.

During the past few seasons the Indian threat had diminished, though Geronimo's Chiricahua Apaches were still on the loose and only four weeks ago a half-troop of Crook's Fifth Cavalry had nooned at Hat and told of the scalping and burning of a family and homestead just eight miles beyond the town of Arrowhead, only sixteen miles from Hat headquarters.

In the west, the sun slid down over the rim with a brilliant flash of reds and yellows. Then hoof beats crunching the snow echoed through the silence. Ray Queene whipped toward the door, but Sebastian restrained him. 'Only one horse. It won't be the doc yet.'

The horseman off-saddled at the steps and mounted the veranda. Sebastian went out to meet him, saying over his shoulder to Queene, 'It's Joe Chess. Wonder what he wants.'

The newcomer's bantam figure crossed the porch into the glow of light spilling through the door. This was Joe Chess, foreman of

Buck DeSpain's ambitious Pitchfork ranch. Sebastian said, 'Evenin', Joe. Come on in. Coffee?'

The little foreman nodded gratefully and pulled off his wool-lined gloves. 'I'm makin' the rounds to find out how everybody made out. Hi, Queene.'

Ray Queene's blond head dipped and he said with exact courtesy, 'Evening, Joe.'

Sebastian wrapped a mitten around the coffeepot handle and took it off the fire. 'What's the damage at Pitchfork?'

'Could be worse,' Chess said. His eyes peered around curiously. 'We managed to pen a big bunch up in Box Canyon. They weathered through all right. Rest of the herd must have dusted south with yours. Where's Parrott?'

'Bed,' Queene said shortly. 'Come down with a fever.'

'That so?'

'Mrs. Parrott's dead,' Sebastian told him.

'No!' The little rider's eyebrows rose. 'They get caught in it?'

'Driving home from Arrowhead,' Sebastian told him. 'Anybody hurt over your way?'

'No,' Chess said. He was a thin little man with tiny eyes and a hooked-up chin; his hands moved restlessly. He accepted a tin cup of coffee from Sebastian and whirled to face the door.

'Somebody coming,' Chess said.

16

Sebastian walked with long-legged strides to the door. Ray Queene was beside him when he went out. 'That's Lucio and the doc,' he said. 'Thank God. Who's that with them?'

'Dan McGarrity,' Sebastian said.

'The deputy?' Joe Chess asked. 'What's he doin' here?'

'One way to find out,' Sebastian told him. 'Ask him.'

The three riders dismounted simultaneously and stepped to the porch, the doctor in the lead. 'Straight on through, Doc,' Sebastian said, and the doctor took his little satchel into the house. The others followed him inside.

Sebastian said, 'Good work, Lucio. Coffee's on the table.'

The cowboy nodded and headed that way, peeling off his coat. Joe Chess was saying, 'What brings you out, Deputy?'

'Just thought I might be able to help somewhere,' Dan McGarrity said. He was young and stocky and sandy-haired, and wore his dented badge proudly. McGarrity said to Sebastian, 'Kelcy's bringing some supplies out in a buckboard. Lucio told us the Parrotts got wrecked in the storm, and we figured you'd need some grub.'

'Much obliged,' Sebastian told him. 'Your sister will do to ride the river with, any time.'

'Yeah,' the deputy said, grinning.

Ray Queene walked back into the dark corridor, was gone a brief while, and came back into the room frowning. Sebastian said, 'Let's go out and put those horses in the barn.'

Queene grunted and followed him outside. They led the four saddled ponies into the nearest of the big barns.

'How's Jesse doing?' Sebastian said.

'You got me,' Queene answered, and followed him into the dark mustiness. 'Nora wouldn't let me in.'

Sebastian lighted a lantern. 'Listen, you see any cows on the north range, crossing back from Dragoon Springs?'

'Not a one,' Queene said, coming out of a stall and firing up a cigarette. Queene screwed up his angular face into a frown and turned out of the barn. 'What's Joe Chess up to? I never trusted that little crook.'

'Beats me,' Sebastian said. They entered the house, and seeing the corridor door closed, sat down to wait.

'That wind,' Joe Chess allowed, 'had Texas dimensions.'

Deputy Dan McGarrity grunted. Sebastian poured a fresh cup of coffee. Waiting pulled his nerves tight, and he paced the room with a confined man's restlessness until finally Ray Queene told him, 'Sit down. Wearin' a trench in the floor ain't going to help anybody.'

He sat. On the way through the corridor, hours earlier, he had seen through the open door of one bedroom a blanket-wrapped figure on a bed; that was Molly Parrott. A slim and almost fragile woman, she had been drawn west from her Louisiana home by a great love for her husband. Not the kind of woman to be found on every ranch, she had kept this rambling, lonely house in order, raised their only daughter, entertained her husband's rough friends at roundup time, mothered the ranch crew and had run off at odd times to any neighbor who needed help. She had been a great lady.

Sundown was long past. Finally the doctor came out of the back of the house, laid a short, blank glance on the group, and said, 'Mind gettin' my horse? Lot of other folks need me tonight.'

'Sure,' Ray Queene said, and went out. The doctor's face was weary.

Sebastian said, 'Doc?'

The doctor was shaking his head gently. 'Pneumonia. He won't last the night. He's sleeping now and I showed Nora how to make him comfortable if he wakes up. I don't think he will. It's a shame, Clay. A crying shame. He was the biggest man I ever knew. God knows what this Basin will come to now.' He cast a single, direct glance at Joe Chess, and went out on the porch. Queene had brought his horse up. The doctor said, 'Good night. I'll send the parson out from Arrowhead.' He gathered up the reins and wheeled his horse out of the yard.

'Well,' Joe Chess breathed. 'Now, how

about that!' With a new light in his small eyes, he walked down the steps into the yard. 'I'd best be goin'. I'm sorry about Jesse. Adios.'

Chess' little figure disappeared into the barn. Sebastian turned back inside. 'Lucio, you better get some shut-eye.'

The cowboy's face was sad. He nodded and left the room. Ray Queene looked at Sebastian. 'Something bad about that Joe Chess. I don't like what I saw in his eyes when Doc told him Jess was dying.'

'Joe Chess is the least of our worries right now,' Sebastian told him. He looked at the portrait over the fireplace and remembered his promise to keep Hat together for Jesse. But the wolves were already starting to gather. Joe Chess had been the first. Joe Chess, foreman, represented Buck DeSpain's Pitchfork, with its tough crew. DeSpain's covetous eye had lain long on Hat's grass.

Sebastian's eyes moved from the painting to the smaller framed parchment beside it on the wall: the original Spanish land grant deed to what was now Hat, bought by Jesse Parrott twelve years ago from Juan Porfiro Ruiz y Ortega. It had cost Jesse four thousand head of longhorns and ownership of South Texas' biggest freight line, but it had been worth it. Now it was up to Clay Sebastian to keep the grant's acres intact.

Ray Queene's eyes were worried. 'I know how Nora must be takin' this. I wish I'd gone ahead and married her last fall instead of waitin'. She needs somebody now.'

'You can still help her,' Sebastian said. 'Just be around when she needs you.'

'I'm around,' Queene said. His tone was half miserable. 'I'm always around.' Nora, who had her ways of being a little too spoiled and a little too selfish, had given Ray more than his share of hard times. Finally, a year ago, she had agreed to marry him; but for her own reasons, some of them coquettish, she kept postponing the wedding.

A buckboard pitched down the road and rocked into the yard. Dan McGarrity, who had sat silent with his coffee all this time, put his sad gaze on the door. 'That'll be my sister,' he said. His deputy's badge twinkled when he got up.

Kelcy McGarrity opened the door without knocking and stepped inside, shaking flakes of snow from her hair. It was long hair, and fully as red as Sebastian's. When she looked up her face was flushed with cold and her blue-green eyes were half-shuttered. 'I'm tired, boys. You'll have to unload yourselves?'

'You bet,' Ray Queene said, and followed Dan McGarrity out to the food-laden wagon.

Sebastian touched the girl's cheek. 'You're half-frozen,' he said, and took her to the fire. 'Sit down.'

She raised her feet off the floor and he tugged off her heavy boots. He said, 'Now get out of that coat and drink some of this coffee.'

With a swallow of hot coffee inside her she began to look as though she were thawing. Her face, delicate but not pretty, smiled up at Sebastian and her hands moved. 'Thanks. I was beginning to think Hat had moved ten miles farther out from town.'

'It's a bitter night,' he said quietly, and put his back to the fire. 'Kelcy, Molly Parrott's gone.'

'I know,' she said, dropping her glance. 'I'm so sorry, Clay.'

'And Jesse's dying.'

'What?' Her face moved.

The doc just left. He said Jesse doesn't have a chance.'

'Oh, God!' she whispered. The door banged open to admit her brother and Ray Queene, bearing full armloads of supplies. The two men tramped through the room and out the cook shack door. Sebastian said, 'I'd better help unload,' and went outside to the buckboard.

When he re-entered the room the girl was still sitting before the fire, her blank gaze pinned on the fluttering flames. She said, 'We're losing something great tonight. Jesse's a symbol, Clay, not just a man.'

'He's just a man,' Sebastian disagreed, 'but he's the greatest man I've ever met.'

She looked up. 'What do you do now?'

'Run Hat. I promised him.'

# CHAPTER THREE

Leaving a gather of seventy steers at Rifle Springs with Lucio and 'Sus, Sebastian headed back toward the Breaks and the roundup crew. These badlands were the most difficult possible area in which to gather cattle, and the work was slow and not rewarding. He and fourteen men combed the Breaks from dawn to sunset and, at the end of that day all the cattle counted at Rifle Springs tallied up to only two hundred and thirty-five head. The Hat crew made its camp on a brushy summit that night, a short mile from the camp of Rob MacKenzie's Pennant outfit. MacKenzie rode over from his fire an hour after sundown and stepped wearily down from his saddle. 'We've picked up eighty-nine head today,' he said in a washed-out tone. 'That makes a hundred and seventy for two days' work. At this rate it'll take me a month to find all my cows.'

'If there are that many left,' Ray Queene told him cryptically.

'Simmer down,' Sebastian said. 'Once we get them started toward home a lot of them will just drift back. They need water and there's no water in the Breaks. Probably by tomorrow they'll start drifting in toward Rifle Springs.'

'I sure hope you're right, Clay,' said old Rob

23

MacKenzie. He had been one of Jesse Parrott's closest friends; had worked for Parrott years before on a trail drive. Sebastian felt that when the wolves gathered to begin preying on Hat, MacKenzie and his Pennant men would be the only help he could count on. He said, 'Your boys seen anything of Lew Kohlmeier's toughs?'

'Not a sign of 'em,' MacKenzie said. 'But don't let that fool you.'

Ray Queene said, 'Where's DeSpain's outfit camped tonight?'

'Five miles down the draw,' MacKenzie said.

'I don't trust that jasper any farther than I can see him,' Queene said.

'Nobody does,' MacKenzie agreed. 'But so far he's done nobody harm. I need sleep. Good night.'

'*Adios,*' Sebastian said quietly, and watched the old man's slouched shape move away.

The roundup crew stirred long before dawn, roping fresh horses out of the hobbled cavvy, saddling and eating a quick breakfast standing up. These were all tough men, the men of Hat, used to working the long hours of daylight and sleeping in snatches when they got the chance.

The expectant hush of dawn covered the rugged badlands. With a number of thoughts idling through his mind, Sebastian gigged his pinto gelding forward and crossed the rim of a rocky bluff, descending along a tortuously

24

looping game trail. As he advanced, the canyon walls rose, restricting the paling sky. The sound of his pony's shod hoofs slammed back and forth against the walls. Somewhere below him an animal, possibly a steer, clattered over rocks, and he gigged the pinto again.

It was when he rode across the dry creek that he found the man's body, lying twisted at the base of a gnarled paloverde shrub.

He tarried briefly before dismounting, searching the close horizons with care. Nothing stirred; he drew his rifle from the saddle boot and stepped down slowly, not relaxing vigilance. The corpse was quite stiff; probably dead only a few hours.

'White man,' Sebastian murmured, and knelt to study the features more closely. 'That's McCann—one of Lew Kohlmeier's boys. Shot with a forty-five seventy rifle. Apaches?'

He stood loosely for a frowning moment, then prowled the area for whatever signs might lie in the cold earth. Heading up the broken slope to the east he found sharply cut tracks of two unshod horses, and one shod animal. Closer inspection of the two sets of tracks revealed that the shod horse had arrived here first.

Sebastian squinted along the dimming back trails. 'Dead man rode in here alone. Indians bushwhacked him from up above, then rode down to have a closer look. But they didn't take his scalp. Maybe something scared them off? They must have been on business—took his horse when they left.'

In the dead man's pockets he found a few gold coins, a clasp knife, a fire-starting flintlock mechanism, a crumpled bandanna, a pipe and tobacco pouch, and, in the waistcoat pocket, a small .32 caliber derringer, loaded and unfired. The man's revolver was missing from its holster. 'They took that, too.' He bounced the derringer in the palm of his hand, frowning darkly. Then he slid the little gun into the top of his boot and rose to his full height. No sound broke the stillness. The rising sun was rapidly warming the land.

He used a knife-sharpened stick to dig. The hard soil made a rough chore of it; the sun climbed and the day's warmth began to crowd down. The great blizzard had marked the last onslaught of winter and now Arizona's spring was advancing with its measured heat. It was mid-morning by the time he was satisfied with the depth of the grave. Presently he laid the stick aside and carried McCann to the grave, rolled him in and filled it with stones and dirt. Two paloverde sticks, tied in a cross with. rawhide thongs from his saddle conchos, made his marker; and then, breathing heavily, he stood over the grave a moment with his hat in both fists. He had hardly known this man, no more than to identify him; he had not known what his dreams were. He shook his head and turned away. It was a lonely moment in a lonely land.

Dull heat commenced to smother the little defile as he went up the slope afoot to try and determine the direction of travel of the two Indians. Then he mounted the pinto, gave the new grave a last, thoughtful scrutiny, and headed the horse up the side of the canyon.

Before he had traveled twenty minutes farther into the Breaks, the muffled sound of hoof beats echoed from somewhere behind, and he wheeled into a stand of mesquites to conceal himself. Bent forward with his hand over the pinto's nostrils, he peered through the mesquite branches at the switchback of his own back trail. Hoof beats sounded louder; Sebastian murmured, 'Two horses, not in any hurry.'

Presently the two horsemen came into view on a distant hogback. They drew rein there, seemed to hold a brief conversation, and split up, one rider going back the way he had come, and the second rider advancing toward Sebastian. Sebastian frowned, squinting to try for a better look at the departing rider.

'I could be wrong,' he said aloud, 'but that looked like Buck DeSpain's big sorrel.'

The approaching rider disappeared from view momentarily and then broke out of the mouth of a gulch, trotting his horse. *Well, now,* Sebastian thought, *that's Lew Kohlmeier.* And he frowned darkly. What strange sort of politics would find Lew Kohlmeier riding at Buck DeSpain's stirrup?

Then again, he reflected, no one had ever been quite sure of what side of the fence Buck DeSpain rode. A moment's conjecture, and the pairing off of the rancher DeSpain and the rustler Kohlmeier no longer seemed out of place.

Kohlmeier's dun advanced, kicking up little whorls of dust; when the man was quite close, Sebastian gigged his pinto out of the mesquites and held his right hand up, palm out, in a gesture of peace. 'Howdy, Lew.'

If his sudden presence surprised Kohlmeier, the rustler's bland face didn't show it. Kohlmeier pulled up and waited for Sebastian to cross the intervening twenty yards. The rustler sat calmly, both hands folded over the saddle horn, and regarded Sebastian with a look of dry and secret amusement. 'Howdy yourself, Clay. Nice day for a ride.'

'I had the idea,' Sebastian observed, 'that you preferred the nighttime for your travel.'

Kohlmeier grinned; he didn't seem ruffled. He was a tall, powerfully built man, with dark, handsome features and white, even teeth. He said, 'Rode past a fresh grave back there. You dig it?'

'Yes.' Sebastian dropped his reins over the pommel to roll a cigarette. 'One of your boys. McCann.'

Kohlmeier's eyes opened a little wider. 'That so? What happened?'

'Apaches. I've been following their trail a little ways to make sure which way they headed. If they're still camped in this bailiwick, I'd kind of like to know it.'

Kohlmeier seemed to be thinking about it. 'You've got a point there,' he said. 'Mind if I ride along with you?'

'Not at all,' Sebastian told him with dry magnanimity. 'Just you ride in front of me.'

Kohlmeier grinned disarmingly. 'Sure enough, Clay.' He picked up his reins and clucked at the dun. Sebastian followed, watching the surrounding summits with care, and sitting his saddle with the slouched ease of long habit.

Through the rest of the morning neither man spoke. They left the Breaks at noon, still following the trail of two unshod Indian ponies and a captured shod horse. In a short while Lew Kohlmeier said, 'Looks like they're aimed straight for Quail Creek Canyon.'

Sebastian peered ahead into the dark risings of the Monarchs. 'Makes sense,' he said. 'That's the nearest water, and the best trail over the mountains.'

Kohlmeier drew rein and waited for him to catch up. 'Well,' Kohlmeier said, 'that satisfies me. They're headed for some other valley by now. Think I'll go home.'

'Hold it,' Sebastian said, and Kohlmeier

29

looked around Sebastian said, 'That storm pushed a hell of a lot of cows down into the Breaks.'

Kohlmeier's brows lifted. 'Did it, now?'

'If I catch you or any one of your boys near a branded steer,' Sebastian said levelly, 'I'll round up every one of you and we'll have a little hangin' party, Lew. You just keep your crew out of the Breaks until this roundup's over.'

The rustler's teeth flashed and he leaned forward, hands at the pony's withers. 'The day I start takin' orders from a Hat cowboy ain't come yet, Clay. Mind your manners.'

But Kohlmeier kept right on grinning at him. 'I'm no gunman, Clay. Just an honest working rancher.' His grin widened and he wheeled his horse off the trail and broke it into a gallop. Sebastian sat his pinto, watching the handsome man drum northeast into the foothills, and frowned after the retreating figure. Lew was likable, damnably likable; under other circumstances Sebastian could easily see himself siding the rustler. But the line had been firmly drawn; and they stood on opposite sides.

He shook his head and reversed his horse, aiming it back toward the rim of the Breaks.

Over the distant peaks appeared the shadowy streaks of rain. Otherwise the sky was cloudless and deep. On the ground, sheltered pockets here and there still held mounds of melting snow. The glare of the white land beat against his eyes. Near the willow banks at the bend of Rifle Creek he turned sharply southeast, planning to comb that part of the Breaks for cattle. His trail skirted the foothills, sidling against the badland cuts and gullies. He topped a treeless bluff and saw below where half a dozen steers had plunged over a cutbank in the storm and died in the gully beneath.

Still scaring up no beeves, he made another turn near the beginnings of the mountains' black, tangled mass. He aimed more directly into the trecherous windings of the eroded Breaks. The land was smoky with heat. It was almost three o'clock by the time he came upon the first scatter of cattle in a sheltered draw; a quick rough tally counted twenty-two head. Closer inspection showed it to be a group of Hat steers, and he went around to the far end of the bunch, waved his hat, whooped, and drove the cattle out of the gully. Then he was kept busy running around both ends of the little herd's drag, keeping the more obnoxious steers moving with the herd instead of away from it.

He had just topped a miniature butte when his pinto shuddered suddenly and fell to its knees; as he was spilling out of the saddle Sebastian heard the echoes of a rifle shot slamming back and forth through the broken gullies. He hit the ground hard on his shoulder and it was experience-born instinct that made him roll immediately to the shelter of the downed horse's body. He reached over the saddle to tug his rifle from the saddle boot, and then removed his hat and cautiously peered over the mount of the horse. Blood welled from a hole below its shoulder; it heaved and wheezed, and stopped breathing. Sebastian cursed and surveyed the horizons. But he had no success until two rifles, widely separated along the top of a low ridge, began talking in harsh, steady signals. Bullets ripped up little ribbons of dust all around him and one thwacked solidly into the dead horse. Sebastian dropped flat behind the pinto and turned his head to search behind him.

'Who the hell is doin' all the shooting?' he said. Fifteen yards away was the lip of a cutbank. If he could make it that far, he might be able to drop into the arroyo beyond, move to one side or the other, and confuse his attackers. As it was now, they could just wait him out. He had to move.

He played possum until the gunfire let up; then he gathered his legs beneath him and broke away from the dead horse with knees pumping, bootheels digging into the ground. He had covered two-thirds of the distance to the arroyo's rim before the first shot went off behind him; he thrust his heels in and went over the rim in a long dive, hoping the arroyo wasn't too deep. He broke his sliding fall with his hands and whirled back to put his back to the arroyo wall. A glance over the lip of it showed him the last of the cattle disappearing around a distant hogback, and twin wisps of smoke rising nebulously from the ridge above. One of those rifles spoke now, once, and then quieted because it had no target. From the sound of it it was a big bore rifle. He thought, *Maybe a forty-five seventy. Could be our Apache brothers doubled back this morning. Or maybe Lew didn't appreciate the warning I gave him. Well, the odds are better now. Maybe I'll just find out.*

The flush of excitement pulled his lips back from his teeth; Clay Sebastian was a man raised in rough country, a man who needed action. It was his willingness to fight hard which, together with his intelligence and knowledge of men and cattle, had made him foreman of Hat.

He sidled through the narrow arroyo, heading north, occasionally taking a quick, careful glance over the rim toward the east to make sure the two rifle snouts were still posted above.

He reached an eastward turn of the gully and grinned at this piece of good fortune. But when he glanced over the lip again one of the rifle muzzles was gone. The other still commanded the district; but the whereabouts of that missing man worried Sebastian. He silently eared back the hammer of his rifle and crept forward more stealthily; at one point he bent to remove his spurs.

It was alertness to vague little signs, currents in the air and strange reactions to nothing he could see or hear, that had often saved him before; he counted on this ability to protect him now as he approached the petering-out mouth of the arroyo and crawled forward to sweep yonder country. Somewhere nearby a man with a rifle was creeping around, intent on no more than getting a clean shot at him. Sebastian grimaced and moved forward another yard.

Brush rattled to his right and his head turned. *Your last mistake, friend,* he thought, and moved silently in that direction. The terrain here was all tiny humps and ditches; somewhere within a few yards of him was one of his ambushers. Bent almost double, he crept forward with the cocked rifle in both hands, ready. Then against the wall of a brief cutbank he stood fast.

It was the faintest of scratches that became his signal. He raised the rifle muzzle an inch and when a man's figure came around the far end of the little cliff, he pulled the trigger.

The rifle bucked in his hands; and ahead of him, the startled face of the breechclouted Indian stared at him. The Apache's mouth dropped open; his head jerked forward and he collapsed, his Springfield rifle dropping from his grasp. Sebastian's lips pulled back in an involuntary, twisted smile that released some of his tension. Then, close behind him, a shot rang out.

He whirled, levering a shell into the rifle chamber.

Not eight yards from him, the second Apache lay belly-down, face in the dirt, a long-bladed scalping knife in his outthrust hand. And behind the Apache, smoke rising from his pistol barrel, stood Ray Queene.

'He must've run out of shells,' Queene said. 'I caught him crawlin' up on you with that knife.'

Queene wheezed and looked at his gun, holstered it awkwardly and sat down solidly on a rock. He tilted his hat back, exposing his unruly mop of blond hair. 'I never shot anybody before, Clay.'

'I'm obliged,' Sebastian said tightly. He walked forward to toe the Indian's body. 'He's dead.'

'God,' Queene said.

'Why are you out here?'

'Been trailin' you,' Queene said. 'Latigo rode into camp this morning, brought a message from town. They're holding a meeting tomorrow morning. Something about Jesse's will. They want you there.'

Sebastian said, 'Who's "they"?'

'Nora and the lawyer, I guess. Latigo didn't say.'

'All right,' Sebastian said. 'Let's bury these two.'

Queene stood up wearily. 'I guess so. Lord!'


## CHAPTER FOUR

Arrowhead was no more than an irregular scatter of brown adobe buildings, without streets or plan. Only a few trees, scrubby mesquites and paloverdes, graced the village. A few hundred yards away, at the intersection of Parrott Creek and the Massacre River, sycamores and cottonwoods grew thick and tall. Sebastian and Queene clattered across the timber bridge. It was a group of Mexican boys, playing in the settlement compound, who first took note of their arrival; they ran alongside Sebastian's walking horse, looking wide-eyed up into his face, calling, *'Es El Rojo—es El Rojo!'*

Sebastian smiled down at them and rode on through the heat and close-lying dust and past hipshot horses sleeping on their feet at the hitch rails before the single bar. Fancy Lee Chaffee, dressed in his broadcloth finery with silver brocade vest, called from veranda of his saloon, 'Welcome, Clay. The town's wide open and full of suckers.'

Sebastian lifted a hand in acknowledgement and rode around Jackson O'Keefe's general mercantile store. By a 'dobe behind the store, an Indian woman stood, short and the color of old copper, staring through strands of disheveled jet hair. When her squinting glance recognized Sebastian her lips widened into a cracked grin. Sebastian thought wryly of the two men who had died yesterday . . . Her people, he thought, and smiled for her. Dan McGarrity, Arrowhead's law, stepped out of the tiny jail and shaded his eyes with a hand, and waved at Sebastian. 'Meeting's already started,' he said. 'Over at Teale's office.'

Sebastian nodded and racked his horse beside Queene's at the blacksmith shop. McGarrity walked up and Sebastian said, 'Geronimo owes me a horse. Couple of bucks shot him out from under me yesterday.'

'That so?' McGarrity said, interested.

'They're both dead,' Ray Queene said shortly, and turned to follow Sebastian around behind the blacksmith shop to lawyer Noah Teale's cubicle of an office. Teale had managed to combine his talents as blacksmith and legal advisor and make a decent living out of them. Sebastian knocked, heard Teale's voice, and entered. The room was close and hot.

Teale, thick-necked and bald, seemed to have been arguing with Buck DeSpain. Sebastian said, 'Howdy,' and paused to accustom his eyes to the room's dimness. There were a good many people present. All the leeches come after Jesse's gone, he thought. Pitchfork's DeSpain; his foreman Joe Chess; Nora Parrott; young, headstrong

Fletch Diedrich of Slash-D; Pennant's Rob MacKenzie; and, of course, the lawyer.

DeSpain and Joe Chess, and even Fletch Diedrich, all gave Sebastian what he took to be a dirty look. He said, 'What the hell is this?'

'We were just arguing about land rights,' the lawyer said imperturbably. His huge figure seemed out of place behind the desk. 'I suppose we'd better fill you in, Clay.'

'I suppose,' Sebastian agreed tightly. He removed his hat, glanced once at Nora, and leaned the point of his shoulder against the wall.

Noah Teale said, 'This is Jesse's will.' He held up a sheaf of papers. 'A lot of it's irrelevant. You can read it when you want to. Basically, it leaves equal shares of Hat to Nora Parrott and Clay Sebastian.'

Sebastian straightened. 'What?'

'You heard me,' Teale said calmly.

Nora looked up at Sebastian. 'Jesse wanted to make sure you'd stay.'

He frowned. 'I gave him my word. He didn't have to do this.'

'He wrote this will months ago,' Teale said. 'Before Nora and Ray Queene became engaged. I guess he thought he was playing Cupid or something.'

The frown remained across Sebastian's face. 'Go on.'

There's one important part of this will. A clause here stipulates that neither heir can sell or otherwise transfer control of his half of Hat without the consent of the other heir.'

Sebastian nodded. Then he looked at Joe Chess and Fletch Diedrich, at Rob MacKenzie and Buck DeSpain. 'What are all these jokers doing here?'

DeSpain said mildly, 'There was some dispute as to what Hat actually consists of, Clay.'

DeSpain's broad face seemed half amused. His hair and mustache were raven black; his nose was a great hook and his eyes were deeply brown. Buck DeSpain was big and fat; but Sebastian had seen him move with surprising alacrity at times. Sebastian said, 'What's that supposed to mean?'

'Most of Hat ain't on patented land,' DeSpain answered, smiling slightly.

'So?'

'It's free grass, Clay. All but a few sections. In plain language, it belongs to any man that can hold it.'

Sebastian spoke through his teeth, 'I've got a Spanish land grant that says you're a liar, Buck.'

Not ruffled, DeSpain was shaking his head. 'Those old land grants are funny things, Clay. Might take you years to prove the thing up in court.'

Sebastian watched him without blinking. 'Are you trying to talk yourself into a fight, Buck?'

Nora Parrott raised her hand. 'Wait, Clay. Buck's telling the. truth.'

'That's right,' Teale agreed. 'Look on this plat.'

Uncertain, Sebastian crossed to the lawyer's desk and bent over the map. Teale said, 'As you can see, Jesse only had clear title to about a dozen sections—Hat headquarters on Parrott Creek; Dragoon Springs; Aztec Canyon and Quail Creek in the Monarchs; and a few sections out on Nine-Mile Flats where there's water—Peyote Wells and Rifle Springs.'

Sebastian straightened, satisfied. 'In other words, all the water on Hat is on patented land.'

'All except the Massacre River and a part of Parrott Creek,' Teale admitted.

Buck DeSpain's grin widened. 'But you just try and keep thirsty cows from that water, Clay.'

'I'll fence those sections,' Sebastian said promptly. 'And starve your own cows for water?'

DeSpain had a point. Under his breath, Sebastian cursed the man's steady grin. 'I've still got that land grant. And you know damn well it's valid.'

'Do I?' DeSpain said innocently. Then his expression sobered. 'Look, Clay. Be sensible. Diedrich and MacKenzie and I have formed a combine. We want to buy those dozen sections

40

of land. Miss Parrott has agreed to sell her half.'

Sebastian looked at Nora. She said, in a low tone, 'It may save a lot of fighting, Clay.'

Sebastian snorted. 'By the terms of the will, you can't sell your half unless I consent to it.'

Fletch Diedrich put in a brief correction, 'Not just your consent, Clay. We want to buy your half, too.'

Sebastian's gaze moved from Diedrich across Rob MacKenzie's leathery face to DeSpain. 'For how much, Buck?'

'Times are hard, with the blizzard wiping out half our herds. Of course, Hat was hit harder than the rest of us. Ain't much left of Hat. We'll go five thousand.'

'For each section,' Sebastian added.

'No,' DeSpain said. 'For the whole works.'

Sebastian laughed in his face. 'You can go to hell, Buck.' He turned on his heel and headed for the door.

Nora's voice turned him around. Her tone pleaded, 'Wait, Clay.'

He turned to see DeSpain rising from his chair. DeSpain's chin tucked in and he said, 'Jesse Parrott built Hat up to what it was, Clay. Jesse used to run twenty thousand head of cattle and Jesse used to pay an eighteen-man crew. But you've got to get it straight in your head, boy. Jesse's dead and your crew's gone, all but you and Queene and a few diehards, and Queene's sidin' with Nora Parrott in this.

41

Maybe you've got a few thousand head of beef left somewhere on Hat, but they're scattered to hell and gone all over Massacre Basin. You got no money and not much crew, and half a million acres of empty land, most of it not patented and under dispute. You used to make big tracks, Clay. But not now. Either you sell out to us or we'll take Hat. The easy way or the hard way. It makes damn little difference to me, boy. Make up your mind.'

Not visibly shaken by the heat of DeSpain's talk, Sebastian stood gravely watching Nora. 'Do you really want to sell out to these greedy wolves?'

She nodded mutely. Sebastian swung to Ray Queene. 'And you?'

'Do you want a range war, Clay?' Queene's look was helpless. 'What else can we do?'

'By God, we can fight,' Sebastian said. 'Teale, you can start making up a case to prove that land grant right now. And Buck, I told you before: You can go plumb to hell.'

'Much obliged,' DeSpain drawled. 'I hope you don't lose too much sleep, boy.'

But Sebastian was already out the door. He walked forward with long strides and was lifting his foot to the stirrup when old Rob MacKenzie touched his arm. 'You sure you know what you're doin', Clay?'

The hot rash of anger had not diminished. 'I'm sure,' Clay told him. 'Now go back and join your jackal *compadres.*'

'Ease off,' the old man said. 'I'm still your friend.'

'That's why you joined Buck's combine in that offer, I suppose.'

'In the offer,' MacKenzie said. 'Sure, I could use some of Hat's grass. But I won't ride with them in a fight. Neither will my boys '

'And you won't ride with Hat either, is that it?'

MacKenzie shook his head. 'I don't know, Clay. We'll have to see about it.' He wandered off, still shaking his grizzled head.

Sebastian cursed and wheeled his pony away from the blacksmith shop. He remembered what Jesse had said on his deathbed. 'When I'm gone the wolves will come out of their black holes and gang up on Hat like a pack after a crippled antelope.' Well, he reflected, the pack's starting.

He dismounted before Jackson O'Keefe, behind the cash counter, looked up. 'Got your mad up, Clay?'

'That I do,' Sebastian breathed. 'Give me a carton of forty-four cartridges.'

O'Keefe reached up to a shelf. 'Think you'll need all these?'

'And maybe more,' Sebastian said. 'Where's Kelcy?'

'Out back,' O'Keefe said. Just then the storeroom door opened and Kelcy McGarrity stepped into the room. Her mass of red hair was so thick it was almost solid. She smiled when she saw Sebastian. Shrewdly, Jackson O'Keefe untied his apron, grinned at the girl and walked out of the building.

Kelcy laughed. 'I think he's trying to promote something.'

Sebastian smiled briefly. 'Come to think of it, that wouldn't be too bad an idea.'

A pair of flour barrels sat in the corner beyond the counter. Kelcy sat on one of them and patted the other in signal. When Sebastian sat, she said, 'All right, let's have it. You never come to see me unless you've got trouble. What is it this time?'

In all the time he had spent in Massacre Basin, Kelcy was the only person he'd ever let see the uncertainties and fears in him. To the rest of the world he was a tall, tough man, and that was all. But now he said, 'They're out to bust Hat.'

'DeSpain?'

He nodded, and told her of the conversation in Noah Teale's office. 'And yesterday I'm pretty sure I spotted DeSpain holding a powwow with Lew Kohlmeier. It adds up to a pretty big pill for Hat to swallow.'

'But you're going to fight them all?'

He raised both hands, palms up. 'What the hell else can I do? My back's to the wall.'

'You could always leave Hat. Sell out'

He shook his head. 'I made a promise to Jesse.'

She frowned at her toes. 'Dan told me that

Nora fired nine or ten Hat cowboys yesterday. She told them Hat didn't have enough beef left to justify a big crew.'

His glance whipped up. 'What? She didn't say anything about it today. She had no right to do that.'

Kelcy shrugged. 'It's done now. What are you going to do?'

'I wish I knew,' he said, standing up.

She said in a musing tone, 'A friend of Fancy Lee Chaffee's is in town. Jeremiah Rivers.'

'Rivers?' Sebastian frowned. 'What's he doing in Arrowhead?'

'Who knows? Maybe the Earps made it too hot for him around Tombstone.'

'And maybe Buck DeSpain's hired himself a gun.'

'I doubt that,' she said. 'Rivers hasn't left Chaffee's saloon since he got here before the storm. Maybe you ought to talk to him.'

'Rivers?'

'Yes.'

Sebastian shook his head. 'I don't hire guns to do my fighting, Kelcy.'

'He might help to even the odds a little.'

'No,' he said, in a thoughtful tone. 'But maybe I ought to go over there and try to find out what his business is here.' He took a step forward.

He turned. Kelcy's arms were lifted and when he moved she bent her head and pulled him down by the neck; he felt the warmth of her lips on his and then she said, quite softly, 'I wish, dammit, that once in a while you'd come around here without bringing your troubles with you.'

'I'm sorry, Kelcy.' He dipped his head for another kiss, turned and left. Outside, in the shade under the veranda overhang, Jackson O'Keefe grinned at him and swung inside. Sebastian walked around the end of the feed stable and tramped the dust to Fancy Lee Chaffee's saloon.

A man on the porch stood up from his chair and swung to face him: Joe Chess. The little man eyed him steadily and silently, then whirled abruptly and left the porch. Sebastian watched him cruise the dust, his spurs dragging the dirt, then turned inside.

The first man he saw was Fletch Diedrich, Slash-D's impetuous young owner. Diedrich swung defensively away from the bar touching his gun butt nervously, when Sebastian entered. Sebastian laughed.

Diedrich said, 'What's so damn funny, Clay?'

'How you ever built an outfit the size of Slash-D I'll never know, Fletch. You're jumpin' at shadows. Calm down—nobody's going to shoot you.'

Diedrich turned back to his drink. His glance sidled toward Sebastian. Sebastian put his belly to the bar and nodded to Fancy Lee Chaffee. Fletch Diedrich's words cut the air.

'You don't walk so high and mighty any more, Clay. Watch who you laugh at around here.'

'Calm down,' Sebastian said. Diedrich talked a much larger brand of toughness then he owned; now he walked half the length of the bar to stand quite close to Sebastian. 'Maybe you didn't hear me, Clay.'

Sebastian turned to watch him blandly. 'Fletch, I've got no fight with you. Not yet. Just stay away from Buck DeSpain and his land-hungry friends, and you'll get along all right. Otherwise Leila's bound to be a widow. Get some sense in your head, kid.'

Diedrich was shaking his head violently. 'You don't give the orders in Massacre Basin any longer, Clay. But I guess you may have to learn that the hard way.'

'I guess so,' Sebastian said very quietly. 'Now get the hell out of here before you talk us into a fight that neither of us wants.'

'What?' Diedrich had his hackles up, Sebastian saw. The man's hand dropped from the bar and on that signal Sebastian's own fist whipped forward, caught the gun out of Diedrich's holster and tossed it across the room. Grunting, Sebastian lifted Diedrich by the back of his shirt collar and the seat of his pants, and rushed him out the door. When he let go, Diedrich fell across the porch and sprawled roughly in the dust. Diedrich rolled over and said thinly, 'That was a mistake, Clay.

A bad mistake.'

'Go home,' Sebastian said wearily, and swung back inside the saloon. He heard a man's low chuckling and looked back, and saw in a dim corner the shape of a stranger sitting at a table. Fancy Lee Chaffee moved behind the bar. 'Maybe he was right, Clay. Maybe that was a mistake. You sure put a dent in his pride just now. I'd watch my back from here on out.'

'I don't worry about Fletch,' Sebastian said. 'He takes his orders from Buck DeSpain.'

'Maybe,' Chaffee said cryptically.

'I want to talk to Jeremiah Rivers,' Sebastian said.

Chaffee's eyebrows went up. 'You sure about that? Well, he's—'

'Right here,' said the stranger in the back corner. He rose and came to the bar.

Dressed entirely in buckskins, he was a tremendously tall, tremendously thin man, with deep black eyes set wide apart and a mane of thick black hair. The points of his long mustache dropped around his lip corners. Jeremiah Rivers wore a pair of polished Colts in matched, tied-down holsters low along his thighs. 'That was a sporting game you just played, cowboy.'

'This is Clay Sebastian,' Chaffee said. 'He ramrods Hat.'

'Or he used to,' the gunfighter murmured. 'So I hear.'

'Just one question,' Sebastian said. 'What's

48

your business in Massacre Basin?'

'Why,' Rivers said, 'I'd suppose it was exactly that, Mr. Sebastian. My business.' He didn't seem roused.

'I like to know if a man has been hired to gun me,' Sebastian said. 'I like to see his face.'

Rivers smiled a gentle, lonely smile. 'If I were being paid to pick a fight with you, Mr. Sebastian, I'd have picked it by now.'

'Then you weren't hired to bird-dog Hat?'

'I didn't say that,' Rivers murmured. 'Then again, I might deny it. Let me put it this way. I came here to do a job I found the storm had done for me. Now I'm waiting for further orders from the man who's paying my salary. Is that enough, sir?'

It was, Sebastian realized, as close to the truth as the gunfighter would get. He said, 'It'll do. I expect that sooner or later you'll be calling me out. Just remember one thing, Rivers.'

'What's that?'

'You don't know this country as well as I do,' Sebastian said, and wheeled to the door.


## CHAPTER FIVE

From what Jeremiah Rivers had implied, it seemed plain that someone had paid him to kill Jesse Parrott. This in turn meant that someone, probably Buck DeSpain, had been planning this move against Hat for some time, and that the sudden blizzard had been only a piece of good luck for him, and not the beginning of his plot Proceeding from that assumption, Sebastian knew that it would be only a matter of time before Rivers would be camping on his trail.

He cursed under his breath and tramped out onto the veranda, looking out into the fast Hat yard at the small group of cowboys gathered there. 'Lucio, 'Sus, Latigo, Shorty Palumbo, Sandoval. You, Ray, and me. It doesn't amount to much of an army.'

'That it don't,' Queene agreed blandly.

'You killed one man a few days ago,' Sebastian said.

'He was an Indian,' Queene objected.

'You may have to shoot at more men before this is over. Willing?'

'Willing to try,' Queene said. 'I've got more of a stake in this than any of the other boys.'

'I suppose you do,' Sebastian admitted, remembering that before this ruckus had started, Queene had been planning to marry Nora Parrott. 'The first thing you had better do is hitch up the wagon and drive Nora into town. She can stay with Kelcy McGarrity. I don't want her here if bullets start flying.'

'I already asked her,' Queene said. 'She won't go.'

'That's right.'

Sebastian turned his head and saw Nora in the door behind him. She said, 'I was a fool to think we'd stop anything by giving in to DeSpain.'

Sebastian nodded. 'Give a man like that an inch and he wants the whole mile. You can't be soft with Buck. But I still want you in town, where it's safe.'

'Who knows where it will be safe?' she said. 'Clay, I was born in my father's house. Not this one, but one like it. I'm not leaving my own place now. Besides, I can use a gun. You taught me.'

Sebastian grunted. 'All right. But if anything starts, you get down in the cold cellar and bar the door.' He turned to face the small gathering of Hat punchers. 'You boys are all that's left of the crew. DeSpain has seven men; Diedrich has eight or ten more; and they may have Kohlmeier's toughs with them. That makes the odds longer than I'll ask anybody to face. If you want to quit you're free to go. Draw your pay now.'

The five men milled a little, all looking at each other, at Queene, at Nora, at Sebastian. Lucio stepped forward. 'We will stay.'

Sebastian let out a long breath. 'All right,' he said. 'Oil your guns and keep them ready.' He swung inside the house.

Queene and Nora followed him. Sebastian said, 'Maybe you both ought to clear out. No telling what's going to happen.'

'Be serious,' Queene said. 'What do we do now?'

'Finish what we started,' Sebastian said. 'I doubt DeSpain will move until he gets Diedrich's crew organized with his own. We'll leave two of the boys here with Nora, and get back to the Breaks. I want to get as many head of Hat beef back on Hat range as I can before Kohlmeier combs the Breaks dry.'

'Sounds as good as anything,' Queene said listlessly.

'Saddle up, then.'

'Wait,' Nora said. 'Someone's coming.'

Sebastian went to the door and opened it. 'Joe Chess,' he grunted. 'Alone.'

The bantam Pichfork foreman rode into the yard with no perceptible hurry, right arm held high. He called, 'I'm not wearin' a gun.'

'Step down, then,' Sebastian said, and descended the veranda steps to meet him. Chess did not dismount.

Chess grinned at him with his beady stare. 'Brought you a message. Buck's gatherin' a herd on Arrowhead Flats. We're goin' to push them onto Hat morning after tomorrow.' He lifted his hand in sardonic signal, turned and rode away as mildly as he had come.

'Makin' a brag,' Ray Queene said, surprised. 'What the hell was that for?'

'It's a slap in the face,' Sebastian said. 'He's throwing down our challenge. He'll have every rider he can muster with that token herd,

52

moving a few head of Pitchfork beef onto Hat. If we let him do it, we're done. If we fight, they'll have the advantage. Buck wants us to fight.'

'And what'll we do?' Queene said.

'We'll see,' Sebastian said, 'Take 'Sus and Latigo down to the Breaks with you and start bringing those cattle out.'

'Where are you going?'

'To Slash-D,' Sebastian said. 'Maybe I can still talk some sense into Fletch Diedrich. He's not bad, just mixed up. He follows DeSpain's lead because DeSpain talks tough. Maybe I can talk him out of it. Without the Slash-D crew, DeSpain won't look quite so tall when he crosses the line onto Hat with those cows.'

'It's a long chance,' Queene told him.

'But worth a try.' Sebastian crossed to the corral to rope out and saddle a mount.

When he was stepping into the saddle, Queene came down to grab his bridle. 'I heard what you did to Fletch in Chaffee's yesterday. He ain't going to take kindly to peace talk from you, Clay.'

'I can try,' Sebastian said again, and left the corral. Slash-D was a good many miles southwest and he moved along, now walking the horse, now galloping, now trotting. He splashed twice across loops of the Massacre, rode through the riverbank timber and broke out onto the open plain on what was commonly agreed was the beginning of

Slash-D's grass. Or had been up to now. Sebastian grimaced.

A rider was quartering across the plain from the direction of Arrowhead, raising a little banner of dust, and Sebastian observed that his own path would converge with that of the rider. He shrugged and touched his gunbutt, and rode on.

When the rider moved closer he recognized Montez, one of Diedrich's hands. Montez was a 'breed, young and full of fire, just the sort of man Diedrich would pick to work for him. That was why Diedrich needed more cowboys to handle the same number of cattle. He picked fighters, not cowmen. Just now Montez intersected his path and galloped forward. Sebastian swung in the saddle to keep his glance on the man.

' 'Mornin,' Montez said idly.

Sebastian nodded; his eyes were narrowed. to slits, but there was a gleam behind them. He didn't trust this man at all. He said as much. 'Mind ridin' ahead of me, cowboy?'

Montez was ruffled immediately. He drew up in the saddle and flashed an intense glance at Sebastian. 'Is that your roundabout way of callin' a man a back-shooter?'

'Just taking no chances,' Sebastian said.

Then Montez grinned and shrugged. 'I reckon it don't make no difference. You'll be washed up in forty-eight hours anyway. Soon as we push that herd onto flat grass, you're done, Sebastian. All done.'

'Go on, cowboy.'

Montez gigged his horse to take the lead; but Sebastian saw a new light, partly speculative, behind the man's blandness of gaze. When Montez went past, his right arm was concealed from Sebastian's view. It was then that the 'breed decided to make his draw. Sebastian saw his elbow rise; he lifted his own revolver and was earing back the hammer when Montez threw his gun under his left arm. Sebastian saw the muzzle coming up and let his own thumb slip off the hammer. The gun rocked and Montez lurched in the saddle; startled by the shot, the cowboy's horse jerked away and galloped a few yards, spilling Montez out of the saddle, and came to a halt nearby, cropping grass.

Sebastian's lips pulled back and he punched the empty cartridge case out of his revolver, and reloaded. Then he dismounted and walked to Montez, and knelt.

The man was dead. Sebastian felt his belly chugging. He holstered his revolver, stood up slowly and went to get Montez's horse. The man was a heavy burden; he put the body across the saddle, picked up the reins and rode forward.

*That's two men I've shot inside a week,* he thought. *God, isn't it enough?* He remembered Ray Queene's lurching reaction after Queene had shot the Apache. Sebastian had felt the same way himself; but habit made him keep his eyes narrow and his jaw tense and his face tough. If his enemies ever discovered a soft spot in him, he would be all though.

He led the cowpony with its sagging burden into the Slash-D yard and dismounted. He didn't have to go to the door; Diedrich stormed out before his foot had touched the ground. 'Who's that—who's that?'

'One of yours,' Sebastian said. 'He tried to gun-shoot me.' He felt tired.

'Why,' Diedrich breathed, 'you dirty, back-shootin' killer.'

'The hole's in his front,' Sebastian said calmly. 'Look, Fletch. I didn't pick the fight.'

'I'll bet,' Diedrich said tightly, and raised his voice. 'Gene, come up here!'

A stocky puncher rounded the barn, hesitated when he saw Sebastian, and then came on. 'Help me get him down,' Diedrich said.

The cowboy gave him a hand. He looked dispassionately at Sebastian. 'You shoot him?'

'He forced it.'

The cowboy nodded. 'He had it comin' one day.' And went back around the barn.

Diedrich turned to Sebastian. He settled his feet and shoulders and pointed an unsteady forefinger. 'Now. Just what right have you got to come bustin' in on my land and shootin' one of my boys?'

'Simmer down,' Sebastian said. 'I came over

56

to talk to you, Fletch.'

Diedrich looked down at Montez. 'We ain't got much to talk about, you and me. Not after this.'

Sebastian shook his head. It was a good sign that Diedrich hadn't made a move toward his gun; perhaps the man would listen to reason. 'I didn't pick the fight with him, Fletch. He probably figured if he wiped me out now you'd have less trouble afterward.'

'He was probably right.'

'But it didn't work,' Sebastian said. 'Montez is dead now. How many more people do you want to have to die just because you and Buck DeSpain got greedy?'

Diedrich looked up. He didn't answer. Sebastian said. 'DeSpain's been on the fringe ever since he settled here. Everybody knows he works hand-in-glove with Lew Kohlmeier, stealing beef not only from Hat but from you and MacKenzie and everybody else in the basin. DeSpain's a crook, Fletch. I don't think you are.'

'I won't side Hat,' Diedrich said flatly. 'Hat made me crawl too damn long. I'm tired of playin' second fiddle.'

'Ah,' Sebastian said softly, shaking his head. 'Buck DeSpain put that in your head. We never made you crawl, Fletch. And I'm not asking you to side Hat. Just stay out of it and let me fight this out with DeSpain without interference.'

57

Someone was talking softly behind him. He whirled. But it was only Diedrich's wife. Diedrich said, 'Get back in the house, Leila.'

She was tall and big-boned but still pretty; she said, 'I heard what you said, Clay. Fletch, he's right. This isn't our fight. We've got as much land as we can handle right now. Can't we avoid bloodshed?'

Diedrich was looking worried. 'DeSpain would never let me back out now.'

'What could he do about it?' Sebastian said. 'He can't fight Hat and Slash-D all at once.'

'I don't know,' Diedrich said. His head was down. 'Besides, everybody knows what you did to me in Chaffee's yesterday. Am I supposed to forget all about that?'

'Why not?' Sebastian asked. 'I'll forget it. I already have. To save your own neck, Fletch, and those around you, stay out of this fight.'

Diedrich walked a slow circle around the yard, kicking up little balls of dust. When he came back he said in a low voice, 'I don't know, Clay.'

Sebastian turned and mounted his horse. 'I'm sorry about Montez. Sincerely. Listen, Fletch, DeSpain's going to be pushing a herd onto Hat day after tomorrow. There's going to be a lot of gunfire over there. Just pretend you don't hear a thing.'

'Buck will want to know where I am long before then. I'm supposed to meet him tomorrow with my crew.'

58

Sebastian began to think he had the man moved. 'I guess you'll just have to tell him, Fletch,' he said quietly. There was no easier way.

'Yeah,' Diedrich murmured. He looked up, 'All right, Clay. I reckon you're right. It ain't my fight.'

'Sure, Fletch. Much obliged.' Sebastian turned and rode at a trot out of the yard.

This put a new light on things; with Diedrich hanging back, Hat might yet win out against DeSpain and Kohlmeier. For the first time in days, Sebastian allowed himself to relax with a small smile.

It was sundown by the time he splashed across the Massacre; and on impulse he turned northwest, instead of east toward Hat. It might prove valuable to get the scent of the wind on Pitchfork. A low, ragged ravine enclosed him with steep and wooded slopes; then he was out on the rising prairie above the river, with the night's black becoming thick and solid. Far to the east, the peaks of the Monarchs were high and sharp silhouettes. Noises cut abruptly through the night and he wheeled out of the trail into the higher timber.

The sound of advancing horses grew quickly and he stopped on a high roll of ground to look down through the trees. The moon was just beginning to come up over the Monarchs. He dismounted and. moved to stand by his horse, hand over its nose. Rising interest compelled him to lean forward and study the trail below with care.

A group of riders broke out of the trees and drummed up the trail toward Pitchfork. They seemed quite businesslike, throwing out guards and flanking riders to cover their main party; there were, he guessed, eight or ten in all.

The sudden clatter of hoofs died and Sebastian put his horse back down to the trail to follow the group ahead.

He couldn't be sure but he thought it had been Slash-D, with Fletch Diedrich in the lead. It worried him; he put his horse up the side of a coulee and left the trail to cut straight overland toward Pitchfork. He wanted to be there when Fletch rode in, to find out what was in the young man's impetuous mind.

When he dismounted in the grove of willows near the Pitchfork yard, he was sure he was a good ten minutes ahead of Slash-D. He tied the horse to a branch and crept forward to the rim of the trees, from which it was a short thirty yards to the nearest fence of DeSpain's corral. There was a swift, low run of talk around the yard and after a few minutes' careful observation he thought he had counted fourteen or fifteen men scattered around. He frowned until one high shape moved confidently past the light spilling through a window: Lew Kohlmeier. The rustler's crew had joined forces with DeSpain. Under his breath Sebastian heard the sibilant mutter of his own curses.

The sound of approaching riders grew louder; the men in the yard dispersed into the shadows and Buck DeSpain walked blockily forward to stand in the middle of the yard. A hail ran forward from the advancing horsemen and DeSpain said clearly, 'All right. It's Slash-D.'

The men in the yard emerged from the shadows and then Diedrich rode in at the head of his crew. Sebastian heard DeSpain's voice. 'You weren't supposed to come until tomorrow.'

'I rode over to tell you I'm pullin' out, Buck. Don't count on me against Hat.'

DeSpain's hatbrim rose quickly. 'Turned yellow, kid?'

'No. Just sensible.'

Sebastian saw the subtle shifting of the positions of the men afoot in the yard. They were putting Slash-D in the line of a murderous crossfire, should shooting start. Sebastian wondered if Diedrich saw that. DeSpain said, 'You had to bring your whole crew over here just to tell me that?'

'That's right,' Diedrich said. He pointed at Kohlmeier. 'What's he doing here? I thought you said he was out of this.'

'We need every gun we can get when we move on Hat,' DeSpain said. 'By tomorrow afternoon we'll have a herd together. We move at dawn the day after. Hat knows we're coming.'

'Well,' Diedrich said, 'don't count on Slash-D.' He lifted his reins.

'Hold it.' Lew Kohlmeier's words were crisp and sudden. 'If you want to go home and hide under the bed, kid, then we don't want you with us any more than you want us. But we need your crew. Leave them here—we'll feed them.'

'My crew goes with me,' Diedrich said.

'Then they're all dead,' Lew Kohlmeier said quietly. His tall shape stood with wide stance.

Diedrich brought the back of his hand slowly across his lips and said with measured care, 'Nobody wants to start shooting, Lew. I'm just riding out of here. That's all.'

Sebastian lifted his revolver and balanced it across the limb of the tree, lined on Kohlmeier's belt buckle. But Kohlmeier stood fast, arms folded across his wide chest. Buck DeSpain said, 'I'll remember this, Fletch. Don't ever come to me for help.'

'I don't expect I ever will,' Diedrich said calmly. No one moved when he whirled his horse and Slash-D drummed out of the yard. There was not a word until all sound of their travel had died.

Then Kohlmeier said, 'We're better off without him, Buck. He'd only have turned yellow and run when the shootin' started.'

'I don't like it,' DeSpain said. 'I don't want

him and that 'breed crew of his tom-cattin' around in the brush behind me when I move on Hat.'

'He won't,' Kohlmeier said. 'He'll stay out of it. And there's plenty of time to take care of him. Right now I'd worry about Clay Sebastian.'

'Ah,' DeSpain said, dismissing it. 'Sebastian's got no crew. A hundred says he'll be miles away when we cross his line with our cows.'

'That's a bet,' Lew Kohlmeier said; he grinned and turned away. On that note, Sebastian swung into the timber and walked softly back to his horse.

## CHAPTER SIX

After he rolled into his blankets he lay smoking a cigarette, watching the wispy smoke curl dimly toward the bunkhouse ceiling. Across the room a lamp flickered and the building's mild stove heat made him drowsy; nonetheless he lay awake trying to find a solution to the problems the past days had thrown against him. Diedrich had surprised him tonight; the Texan had faced DeSpain and Kohlmeier with more firmness and less bluster than Sebastian had ever before found in him. It was certainly a piece of good fortune; but

Hat needed more than that. He was beginning to believe the only thing that would help Hat now would be a miracle. But whatever miracles evidenced themselves would have to be performed by Hat.

He turned his thoughts to the meager collection of assets Hat could count on. From what old Rob MacKenzie had said in Arrowhead yesterday, it was plain MacKenzie felt the whole situation was too big and too dangerous for him to chance risking his crew. So there would be no help there. The law, such as it was, was represented in Massacre Basin only by McGarrity. The deputy was young and without much experience; he was brave enough but he was only one man, and his badge wouldn't make men like DeSpain or Kohlmeier hesitate to ride roughshod over him. Furthermore, the claims Hat held on its grass were under dispute, and until that dispute was settled, the deputy's hands would be tied. The law couldn't prevent a man from pushing his cattle onto the free grass of open range.

Arrowhead itself would have to be thinking that after this contest was over, the town would be existing only if the victor in this struggle continued to patronize it. The town would just sit back and watch, and wait. It could not afford to involve itself. The smaller ranchers and homesteaders west of Arrowhead would be in the same predicament, since now they only remained by sufferance of the larger powers. He would find no help there either.

He found himself wishing he had Kelcy McGarrity to talk it out with. But Kelcy was sixteen miles away in town.

Outside, a breeze softly roughed up the leaves. Smoke from his cigarette lay in a film under the ceiling and he stood up, grunting, and crossed the empty room to pour himself a cup of cold coffee. He glanced through a window. Nothing stirred; the moonlit prairie glimmered and dust around the moon was a soft ring. Uncertainty closed in, condensing around him; he wanted to find a way of avoiding the responsibility of throwing his men into a fight that some of them might not live through. But it was fight or quit; there was no middle ground.

He paced around the room, tracks of dry sweat staining his cheeks; he whirled back to the end of the long room, cupped his hand to blow out the lamp, and went back to his bunk. He felt crowded, and disliked the feeling with an intense anger. His lips tightened and he thought, *Time's getting short.* Somewhere in the course of the next twenty-four hours he would have to decide what to do about Pitch-fork's move against Hat. Then he thought of Buck DeSpain, a big fat man with his face broiled lobster red and his shrewd, hungry eyes lying across the line on Hat. DeSpain was eager for land, eager for power—perhaps too eager.

There might be a way of turning the man's intense greed back on him. But if there was a way, what was it?

Including himself he had seven men on Hat. None of them were trained fighters, but all of them were willing to do battle with DeSpain. If there were only a way of peeling Kohlmeier away from Pitchfork, as he had done with Diedrich, Hat might have a chance. But Kohlmeier and DeSpain understood each other too well. DeSpain was using Kohlmeier, and both men knew that. Both men knew also that as soon as Kohlmeier's usefulness came to an end, so would DeSpain's friendliness to him. But Kohlmeier seemed willing to play the game by those rules. Sometimes Sebastian could not understand at all the motives that drove the young rustler; Kohlmeier's temper was quite changeable and, while sometimes his humor bubbled right at the surface, at other times there was a close-guarded, unbending reserve holding him. Willful energy drove Kohlmeier ambitiously; yet the man was too restless to allow himself to be confined by the social codes of his peers. If there was a weakness in Lew Kohlmeier that might be used as a lever against DeSpain, Sebastian couldn't see it.

And so, with a number of troublesome thoughts whirling through his mind, he presently fled into a half-sleep. When he woke and looked through the window, the building was casting a long black shadow against the bright glare of the sunlit background. In a complaining mood, he rose and pulled on his boots and tramped outside to wash and shave. He hung his gun belt over the well's crank handle, sent one direct glance toward the silent house, and bent over the bucket to splash water in his face. Just then a set of hoofs sent their rataplan along the ground, and alertly he moved to stand by his gun. A rider topped a high roll of ground and advanced with a sauntering gait and Sebastian saw it was Ray Queene.

Queene dismounted at the corral, unsaddled quickly and then, leaving his saddle slung across a fence rail, walked up into the yard. Sebastian said, 'What happened?'

Queene seemed troubled. 'I'm not sure,' he said. 'I saw that Jeremiah Rivers gent cruisin' around the Breaks last night and it set me to thinking.'

'What about?'

'He made it plain he was looking for somebody,' Queene said. 'He sat on his horse for a good ten minutes scouting our camp, but he didn't ride in. After a while he looked satisfied and rode away. I think he was expecting to find you down there.'

'Maybe,' Sebastian said. He moved back to the well and worked up a lather to shave.

Behind him, Queene said, 'I thought you ought to be warned.'

67

'I'm warned,' Sebastian said shortly.

'Well,' Queene observed, 'you don't have to jump all over me. What's eatin' you?'

Sebastian's back straightened; he turned around and met Queene's curious glance, and suddenly smiled briefly through the lather. 'Nothing. Sorry—let it pass.'

'Sure,' Queene said. He hesitated a moment, then walked uncertainly toward the main house. Sebastian finished shaving and returned to the bunkhouse to find a clean shirt. Then he cooked up a quick meal, ate rapidly, and washed his utensils at the well. It was almost nine o'clock. Queene came out of the house with Nora and the two of them descended to the yard, not talking; both of them wore worried expressions. Sebastian felt trapped. Queene said, in an idle tone, 'We've got about three thousand head bunched at Rifle Springs. A lot of beeves are starting to drift in toward the water.'

'Keep at it,' Sebastian said. 'I'll ride down with you.'

Nora was obviously perturbed this morning. Whatever patience the girl had was worn ragged. She said, 'Jesse would never have let this happen, Clay. Can't you do something?'

'Jesse's dead,' he said bluntly. 'Nora, you were the one who wanted to give in to DeSpain, and got him all fired up to take Hat. You were the one who fired more than half our crew and left us sitting here with our pants down. Now, maybe I'm willing to forget that much because I made a promise to Jesse. But either you stop feeling sorry for yourself and try and make yourself into half the fighter your father was, or you clear out of here and let us run this without your interference. We don't need your whining.' It was harsh talk and he meant it to be; the girl had been spoiled too long and it was time she was shocked into recognizing reality.

She put her eyes down and didn't answer; he wasn't sure whether he had made his point, and so he said, 'This is the real thing, Nora. You've never seen a range war. If you don't stiffen up now, you'll be in for more grief than you can imagine.'

He turned on his heel and said to Queene, 'Let's ride.'

Queene walked forward at his shoulder, speaking softly. 'That was kind of hard on her, Clay.'

'She's got to toughen up fast,' Sebastian said.

'Maybe. Hold it—someone's coming.'

It was a group of riders, coming up the bank of Parrott Creek from the east. Sebastian frowned. He recognized none of the three tough-looking men, and eastward was not the direction of Pitchfork. Then his frown deepened. 'The one in the lead—that's Cliff Slade. I've seen him once or twice in Kohlmeier's camp, but he doesn't work for

Lew.'

'They're all toughs,' Queene said. 'Now, what . . . ?'

The three men rode right into the center of the yard without slackening pace, and pulled their lathered mounts up on their haunches. The leader, Slade, was big and burly with a thick curling mop of brown hair and whisker-blue jowls; he laid his hard glance flatly against Queene and Sebastian and said, 'Which one of you cowboys is Queene?'

'I am. What of it?'

'I hear you've been talkin' about me.'

Queene said, 'What?' His face was startled.

Sebastian's shoulders settled. He watched the three riders quickly fan out into a wide triangle. This man Slade wasn't very bright and his tactics were transparent as glass. He had been sent to pick a fight, that was all. But why with Queene? Why not with Sebastian?

Queen said, 'Mister, I don't even know who in hell you are.'

Slade was doing a strange thing; he was unbuckling his gunbelt and hanging it across his saddlehorn. 'You're callin' me a liar?' he said in a stubborn tone.

'The hell!' Queene objected.

Sebastian touched his arm. 'We won't talk our way out of this, Ray. Slade came to pick a fight.'

But he knew at that instant that he had made a mistake. He had for that brief moment

70

taken his attention off the two flanking riders; and that was all they had needed. Both their guns were drawn, trained on him and Queene; and now one of them, short and wizened, stepped stiffly down from his saddle and walked across the yard to Nora Parrott, where he stood with the muzzle of his gun waving casually in her direction. The other man, taller and more rugged of feature, gigged his horse forward until he had practically run Sebastian down; and sat there, his gun trained on Sebastian, saying, 'You keep out of this, cowboy. It's a private argument.'

Then the man reached down with his left hand and lifted the revolver from Sebastian's belt. With a gun on his back, and another gun on Nora, he couldn't do a thing. He stood fast, anger rising hotly in his chest. Gently, the big man Slade was dismounting and walking forward. 'Take your belt off, Queene. I want this clean.'

Queene looked at Nora, and at Sebastian, and then at the two armed toughs. Grudgingly he reached down, unbuckled his gun belt and let it drop. Behind him, Sebastian heard the mounted man's soft words. 'Step away from that gun, cowboy.'

Sebastian felt the gun prod his back; he walked several yards away from Queene's gunbelt and stood glaring at Cliff Slade.

Queene said, 'What the hell is this all about?' His voice gave away his mounting apprehension; it climbed shrilly.

Slade grinned through yellow teeth. 'You been tellin' lies about me around the territory, cowboy. I got to teach you a lesson. Nobody calls Cliff Slade a crook.'

'Hell,' Queene said, with a great gust of breath, 'I never even heard of you.'

'Stop talking,' Sebastian told him. 'Listen, Ray. He's big and clumsy and slow and stupid. You can lick him. Don't let him put the sign on you.' But he knew it was no good; fright was already imbedding itself in Queene. Queene was a young and usually lighthearted man who was no fighter; faced with a rugged tough like Slade he was lost. Sebastian forced down his own groan.

Slade had come to a halt three paces from Queene. He stood with his legs bent, one ahead of the other, and his arms hanging relaxed at his sides. His arms and legs had huge girths. He said, 'All right. Come ahead, cowboy.'

Sebastian thought; *Let him start it, Ray.* But he didn't speak. Again he felt the gun barrel touch his shoulder blade, a reminder of the watchful guard behind him. Half across the yard, Nora said, 'Wait!' and took two running steps forward before the man guarding her caught her arm and whirled her roughly.

'Stay put,' the man said in a harsh tone. He raised his gun menacingly,

'Why, you—' the girl began.

72

'Shut up,' the man said. His lips pulled back from his teeth; he struck her lightly across the arm with his gun barrel. Sebastian felt his fists clench; but the man behind him cocked his revolver and those rapid clicks halted him in his tracks. 'You stand hitched, too, cowboy,' his guard said mildly.

All this time panic had been rising visibly to Ray Queene's cheeks. Slade, big and sloppy and dangerous, just stood grinning stupidly at him. 'Come ahead,' he murmured and half-lifted one fist.

Queene broke. He let out a tight little scream and plowed forward against Slade, arms windmilling and head down. Slade stopped him like a wall. The big man's fists pounded straight through Queene's thin arms, reaching his chest, reaching his face. Sebastian saw Queene's head rock back and then Slade's bootheel slammed down against the smaller man's instep. Queene howled and doubled forward; and Slade brought his knee up sharply into Queene's face. Queene rose a foot from the ground and fell on his back with a thump that rocked the yard. All this time Slade had not lost his infuriatingly half-witted grin. He walked forward and raised his boot and slammed his heel into Queene's ribs; Queene gasped and rolled weakly aside.

Sebastian felt his legs gathering; he pushed himself forward and heard the clip-clop of the guard's horse behind him. The gun barrel

73

struck him hard at the intersection of neck and shoulder and he felt his whole arm go numb. He stopped and watched helplessly while Slade reached down patiently, still grinning, and hauled Queene to his feet. Slade held him upright with his left hand while he pounded blow after blow into his face. A red film rose again. But again the gun barrel crashed against the side of his head and he felt himself falling.

He hit the ground and tried to lift himself, and could not; he lay sprawled in the dirt and felt the warm ooze of blood along his temple and tried to lift his head to see. His muscles would not respond and he lay with his nose against the ground. Dimly through the roaring in his ears he heard the monotonous pounding of Slade's fist against Queene' battered body, like the regular blows of an ax against soft wood. The world started heaving and Sebastian reached out blindly to grasp at the ground, trying to keep it from turning over and spilling him off. He faintly heard Nora's screams and the curses of her guard, and a hard slap that might have been against Queene or against the girl's face. The ground continued to spin and tilt and his head rocked with pain.

After a while he thought he heard the creak of saddle leather and the receding hoofbeats of horses, but he couldn't be sure. He lay flat and felt his head pound and his stomach lurch, and he blacked out.

# CHAPTER SEVEN

'Clay—Clay!' It was a soft voice drifting through darkness, sometimes nebulously far away and sometimes quite near. 'Clay.' He tried to move, he tried to open his eyes. Slowly feeling was returning to his flesh and he felt the gritty hardness of the ground beneath him. The sun beat hotly against his closed eyelids. Then water, startlingly cold, splashed suddenly against his face and his body twitched, and he opened his eyes, blinking the water away.

'Clay!' When he looked up through the haze he saw the distorted image of Kelcy McGarrity's face. Recognition came first from her mass of brilliant red hair. He groaned and tried to sit up. His head throbbed mightily. He felt gentle hands dabbing his temple with a damp cloth and then she was helping him to his feet. He stood groggily with his head bowed and one arm over her shoulders, leaning heavily on her.

His head cleared slowly and presently he lifted his face to look at her. Kelcy's expression was of anxious concern. She said quickly, 'Are you all right?'

'I don't know,' he said. His tongue felt thick. 'I think so.'

She patted his cut temple with the damp cloth again. He straightened, grimacing with

75

pain, and tried to peer through the bright noon glare. 'Ray—what about Ray?'

'He's hurt,' she said. 'Very badly. Nora and I took him up to the house.'

He lurched forward, only to feel her restraining hand on his arm. 'Wait, Clay. Don't go in there just now.'

He looked around at her. His vision was clearing. 'Why?'

Her eyes dropped. 'He's—a mess, Clay. There's not much left of his face.'

When he lifted his arm to her shoulders he felt her shudder. From the house he heard muffled sobbing, coming through an open window. He said through lips drawn tight, 'Cliff Slade is a dead man. I wonder if he knows that?'

Kelcy was shaking her head. 'Was that who did it?'

'Slade,' he said again numbly. He shook his head, trying to sharpen his thinking, and immediately regretted the action. Pain shot across his forehead like a lancing arrow. His forehead creased and he moved slowly in gentle gait to the veranda and sat gingerly on the steps. Then he put his hands to his head. 'What are you doing out here?'

'I came out to deliver a message.'

'Another warning from DeSpain,' he said in a muffled tone.

'No. From Rob MacKenzie. He said he wasn't sure about the legal ownership of Hat land, and didn't want to get into a fight where he didn't know which side was in the right. But he said he'd have his crew help comb the Hat cattle out of the Breaks, and hold the herds for you until—until this ends, one way or the other.'

'Well,' he muttered dryly, 'That's nice of the old goat.'

'I can see his point of view,' she objected. 'He can't chance sacrificing the lives of his men when he doesn't know what side's right.'

'He ought to know what side's right,' Sebastian said tightly. 'I'm sick of his damned uncertainties. A man can't sit on the fence in the middle of a war. I don't need Rob MacKenzie.'

'You're not talking sense,' she said quietly.

'If you watched Slade pound all the blood out of Ray, you wouldn't make much sense either,' he said. His head was feeling better now but a dull heat of rage was settling down to lock his mind.

Kelcy said, 'Why did that man do this to Ray? Who was he?'

'Slade's a two-bit tough from the Monarchs. Once in a while he rides with Kohlmeier. DeSpain probably picked him for this job because he can't be traced back to Pitchfork.'

'But why did he do it?'

Sebastian sighed. He groped in his pocket and found his crumpled papers and tobacco, and slowly built a smoke. 'It was a warning from DeSpain. His way of sending out the word that he's not bluffing.'

'But this—this is horrible! He didn't have to do anything like this.'

'Buck likes to make sure,' Sebastian said in a flatly angry voice. 'He probably just told Slade to rough up Queene a little. But Slade's idea of roughing up a man is pretty sudden.'

'Why did he pick Ray, and not you?'

'If the man had fought me, it would have been too obvious. Any cow-country jury would have put two and two together and come up with Buck DeSpain. He can't afford that.'

'I see,' she said. She sat beside him and when he looked at her, her face was heavy with thought. She said, 'Then what DeSpain really wanted from this was to make you mad. Mad enough to do something that would put you outside the law, and put him in the right. He's trying to push you into becoming an outlaw.'

'Something like that,' he agreed. 'But if that's what he wants, he's going to get it. I won't rest until I've caught up to Slade.'

'And meanwhile you'll be leaving Hat unprotected and open for them to grab,' she said. Her voice held a note of urgency. 'Don't you see that's just what he wants?'

'Ray's a friend of mine,' he said stubbornly. 'He's been *segundo* of Hat as long as I've been foreman. I owe it to him to get Slade.'

She shook her head, anxiously trying to make him understand. 'Slade's just a tool,

78

Clay. You know it was DeSpain behind him all the time. Why fight Slade? DeSpain is the man behind the trouble. If you go off after Slade, you'll not only leave Hat for DeSpain to grab, but you'll get Slade if you're lucky and not have accomplished anything, really. DeSpain can hire a dozen Slades. If you chase that man you'll play right into DeSpain's hands.'

'I don't know, Kelcy.' He stood unsteadily and climbed to the veranda. 'I'm going to have a look at Ray.'

'I wish you wouldn't,' she said; but he was already inside the house.

When he came out onto the porch again his face looked sick. He was pounding one fist into the other palm stubbornly and when the girl looked up he said, 'This is the first time I've ever wanted to kill a man, Kelcy.'

'I know,' she said quietly. She reached up to take his hand, and drew him down to sit beside her. 'But let yourself cool off for a little while, Clay. If you think about it you'll see I'm right.'

'Ray may never see again,' he said. 'Where's Nora?'

'She rode out a few minutes ago to get the doctor.'

'Funny,' he mumbled. 'I didn't even hear her go.'

She watched him closely. There was a gentle turn at her lip corners. 'You're in no condition to go riding after Slade,' she said. 'Look, Clay, he can wait. Tackle DeSpain first. There's

79

plenty of time for Cliff Slade?'

His face was woodenly grave. Suddenly he dropped his head into the hollow of her throat and said, 'If you ever tell a man I told you this, I'll call you a liar. But I'm scared, Kelcy. Scared green. I don't know what the hell to do. I'm against a wall with loaded guns aimed at me from everywhere I look. And I'm a working cowman, not a gunfighter. What the hell do I do?'

She pressed herself against him, touching her lips to the top of his head. 'Follow your conscience,' she said. Her voice was very mild and very sure.

He got to his feet then and looked down at her with a small smile on his lips. 'Once in a while a man runs short on strength,' he said. 'Somehow you always manage to give me some of yours. How do you do it?'

She said, 'You don't have to make excuses to me, Clay.'

'No,' he said quietly. 'I guess I don't.' He turned away from the house.

'Where are you going?'

'Out to the Breaks,' he said, 'to round up the crew. I want them fresh in the morning. We're going to meet DeSpain at the Hat line. Stay with Ray, will you?'

'Yes,' she said, and stood still, looking very small and strong, while he got his gun belt from the well's crank handle, went into the corral and saddled a powerful roan gelding.

When he rode out of the corral and bent to close the gate behind him, he looked up at the porch. She gave him a brief wave and turned into the house. He lifted the reins and put the roan southeast toward Nine-Mile Flats.

Riding through the crisp air seemed to clear his head. He realized, after the first hot flush of anger wore off, that Kelcy had been right. It bothered him to have to allow any reprieve at all to Slade, but the vicious man's time would come. Sebastian made himself that promise.

The only sounds breaking the stillness were the clip-clop of the roan's hoofs and the gentle tinkling of bit chains. The plain's sweet smell, rising from the new spring grass, became a thick fragrance in his nostrils, and the wind swept his perspiring face, cooling his flesh. His eyes displayed no definite expression but his lips were pulled tight and his cheeks bulged where his jaw hinges were clenched. His hat made an even line across his forehead. In two hours he achieved the northernmost perimeter of the Flats and continued steadily forward over the more stony soil. There was a blaze of feeling in his face when he thought of that single glance of Ray Queene's battered body in the blood-stained bed. East of him, somewhere in that mass of dome- and spire-tipped mountains, Cliff Slade would be hiding out with a stupid grin stamped across his lips. Uncompromising lines set themselves around Sebastian's mouth.

It was past four o'clock when he found the Hat camp deep in the tangled Breaks. He dismounted by the deserted camp-fire and chafed at the wait he would have to endure until the Hat crew rode in for supper. He unsaddled the roan, rubbed it down, and put the saddle back on with loosened cinch, letting the gelding graze at the end of a twenty-foot picket line. Heat closed in and he removed his hat to squeeze sweat from his brow, and settled on his heels with the sun beating against his shoulders. His head still throbbed with a dull ache.

He came to his feet when a horse walked down the narrow draw and rounded the bend into the camp. Sebastian straightened then and speculatively touched his gun.

The rider was Jeremiah Rivers. Dressed in his buckskins, the gunman dismounted without speaking, brazenly putting his back to Sebastian as he did so, and strolled toward the dead fire, where he knelt to pile sticks together and touch a match to them. He spoke in a conversational tone: 'I've spent two days looking for you.'

'So I heard,' Sebastian said. He felt a touch of fear. 'I haven't been hiding.'

'No,' Rivers said. He pulled a twig from the fire and used its glowing tip to light his long, dark cheroot. 'I wouldn't have expected you to hide.'

Rivers was still squatting on his haunches by

82

the fire. Sebastian said, 'You have business with me?' He felt a slight tremor in his fingers and cursed silently.

'Perhaps,' Rivers murmured. He seemed in no hurry. His voice was a confident baritone. When he stood up he did not move suddenly. He said, 'I understand your *segundo* lost a fight today.'

'Now,' Sebastian breathed, 'where would you have heard that?'

'A gentleman named Slade. He passed me in a hurry, headed toward the Monarchs.'

Sebastian put that bit of information back in his head, and then frowned. Why would Rivers tell him this?

Rivers said, 'You believe I've been hired to pick a fight with you and kill you?'

Sebastian said nothing. He knew he had never been in a deadlier position. He did not speak; he did not move; and he tried to keep his expression blank.

Rivers' cheroot had grown a tall ash, and now he tapped it away. His tone was dryly reluctant, 'Do you intend to pick up Slade's trail?'

'In time,' Sebastian said. 'Not just yet.'

'Then my business with you must wait,' Rivers said. He walked to his horse, mounted, tipped his hat courteously and rode into the draw.

It was only when the sound of horse's hoofs had died away that Sebastian realized he had tensed greatly, bracing his muscles against an expected bullet that had not come. He let out a long sighing breath and squatted by the fire; and then frowned. What was the mysterious task Rivers was pursuing?

Only one answer occurred to Sebastian. It might be that Rivers' job was to follow him when he went after Slade, and take up Slade's part in the fight. Slade would be the bait to draw Sebastian into the trap. It was a devilishly clever plan. DeSpain obviously had been counting on his chasing Slade down and killing him. Then Rivers would brace Sebastian, kill him and ride out of the country. The evidence would show that Sebastian and Slade had shot it out, and both men had died. To DeSpain it was probably plain that Slade was too stupid and too crooked to be allowed to continue living. Slade might talk some day, implicate DeSpain in the assault on Queene. This way, both Slade and Sebastian would be out of DeSpain's way, and none of the blame would ever fall on DeSpain.

It was a sobering realization, that when he took up Slade's trail he would have to confront Jeremiah Rivers as well. But he had made a promise to himself, and an unspoken one to Queene, lying almost unrecognizable in the big, lonely Hat house. For a moment he felt trapped by his own promises; but he knew he had to keep faith with them.

The smell of dust clung to the air from

84

Rivers' departure. Riding dust covered Sebastian's clothes and caked his skin. He remembered a town he had once ridden through, somewhere on the trail in Kansas, where the local tonsorial parlor had given him, for two bits, the use of a huge cast-iron tub and buckets of hot water. The tub had been a great curiosity to him; over six feet long, it had almost allowed him to swim. Just now, in the badlands smoky with heat, he thought enviously of men in baths. Bitterness and uncertainties lay tight around his face; he was still remembering Queene, thinking of Slade and Rivers and DeSpain; and the world crowded in around him, close and unfriendly. Dull heat smothered the draw.

Then he stirred, as though scenting possible trouble; and shortly a small group of horsemen filed into the camp—Hat riders.

Lucio, acting *segundo* in Queene's absence, stepped down, nodding to Sebastian, and went immediately to the fire to build it higher and set the coffeepot on, big and dented and fire-blackened. Lucio hunkered there with his hat tilted back off his sweaty dark brow and said, ' *'Tardes.* I see that Rivers *hombre* going north. Was he here?'

'He was here,' Sebastian said, 'Eat fast, boys, and leave your saddles on. We're riding to Arrowhead Flats tonight.'

His announcement was met by five stares of immediate curiosity, but no one asked a question. Sebastian's glance narrowed as he inspected each man singly. Lucio—tough, competent, quiet. Shorty Palumbo—easygoing, willing to fight for the enjoyment of it. 'Sus—short and squat, almost black of complexion, always silent but often dangerous. Sandoval—almost a twin for the lanky Lucio, and just as able a hand. Latigo—out of Texas, a whipcord and rawhide rider who lived, and might be willing to die, for Hat. This was his crew. Gauging their tempers, he decided not to tell them of Queene's beating; or at least not yet. He didn't want them going off half-cocked after Cliff Slade while DeSpain pushed a herd of Pitchfork cattle onto Hat. Kelcy had convinced him that first things had to come first, but he didn't have Kelcy here to convince his crew, and he didn't want them harboring any resentments toward him in the fight that was sure to come.

He squatted beside Lucio to accept a steaming tin cup of coffee, and spoke in a loud voice, 'You heard about DeSpain. Tomorrow morning he's pushing a herd onto Hat, he says. I aim to stop him. There may be shootin' and I won't order anybody into that. Yesterday I offered you a chance to get out. I'm making the same offer again. *Claro?*'

The only man who registered a reaction was Latigo, whose thin lips tightened into a rebuking grimace. Lucio said, 'We told you of our decision yesterday.'

'*Gracias*,' Sebastian said. By this time Shorty Palumbo, youngest rider on the crew and thus the chore boy by mutual, silent decision, had brought fresh steaks from a butchered steer to the fire.

Sebastian said, 'MacKenzie said he'd hold our cattle on Nine-Mile Flats for us, so we'll leave no nighthawks. We all ride tonight.'

Hat ate in silence, quickly; and then, with the weight of the meal heavy in his belly, Sebastian tightened his saddle cinches, climbed aboard the roan, and led his crew into the narrow defile. Shortly thereafter they broke out of the Breaks onto Nine-Mile Flats and opened their mounts up to a mile-eating, ground-drumming canter. They made a stop at Peyote Wells to breathe the horses and another atop a table bluff six miles farther northwest, and finally drew rein in a single ragged rank along the rim of a long saddle overlooking the Massacre River, and beyond that the beginnings of Arrowhead Flats. A mass of blacker dots along the shadowed plain was the slowly milling Pitchfork herd; a quick estimate in Sebastian's head tallied roughly seven hundred head—hardly a massive herd, but still a sufficient token to prove DeSpain's point. A campfire half a mile away was a motionless glow. In a very soft tone Sebastian said, 'Come over here, Lucio.'

Lucio walked his horse forward. Sebastian swung his arm to point along the higher roll of ground at one end of the saddle. 'Put Latigo up there. You take the other peak. The rest of us will fan out along the rim. I want every man's rifle fully loaded before we start the ball.'

'We will not wait for sunrise then?' Lucio said.

'That's right.'

'I see,' Lucio breathed. 'DeSpain has made one big mistake, I think.'

'He has,' Sebastian agreed, grinning tightly in the night. 'Those cows are between us and his campfire. That makes him a damn fool. I count two nighthawks riding the perimeter of the herd, and eleven blanket rolls around the fire. What do you make out?'

'There is one man by the horse cavvy, to the left of the fire,' Lucio said. He squinted and then smiled. 'There is a man leaving his blankets—see him? He is going to the fire for the coffee, I think.'

Sebastian looked that way and nodded. 'DeSpain's got a lot of gall. But I guess tonight he's going to learn a lesson, Lucio.'

Lucio's teeth flashed. 'I feel honored to be his *profesor.*'

'Get the men posted, then. Nobody fires until I shoot. Aim at the ground under the nearest steers—that will start them moving. And once we start, make a lot of noise. I want to drive that herd right through the camp.'

Lucio lifted his reins; but Sebastian

88

frowned. 'Wait. One more thing. Nobody rides down there. We do a lot of shooting and then we ride out the way we came. *Sabe?* I don't want Pitchfork recognizing any of us.'

'*Sí,*' Lucio said softly, and drifted his horse away. Lucio stopped by each man, and one by one Sebastian saw them peel away and ride without hurry to their assigned posts. He saw Latigo's long-barreled Spencer rifle tip up and rest idly in the rider's hands, pointed casually at the sky.

When each man was in position, Sebastian turned to regard the Flats below. The play he was about to begin would, in the long run, prove nothing. All he aimed to accomplish tonight was to scatter the Pitchfork herd and put a touch of fright into DeSpain's ragtag crew. It would serve two purposes: first, it would gain him time—however long it would take DeSpain to round up the stampeded cattle—time in which to map out a campaign against Pitchfork and consolidate Hat's resources, if there were any. Second, it would let DeSpain know in no uncertain terms that Hat was taking up the challenge, that Hat did not intend to quit. Sebastian doubted it would make DeSpain hesitate, but if Massacre Basin knew Hat was still on its feet and fighting hard, Hat might gain a few needed friends.

The click of his Winchester's hammer under his thumb was a loud sound in the night. He took careful aim, directly at the Pitchfork

89

campfire, and then raised the muzzle until he judged it to be high enough to compensate for the eight-hundred-yard range. Then he squeezed off his shot.

Even from this distance he saw sparks scatter from the fire, and he grinned. At this range it had been nothing more than a lucky shot, but it had made its point. Then the five rifles at either side of him opened up. He levered a fresh cartridge into the chamber, aimed at the ground under the foremost of the herd, and emptied the Winchester's magazine as fast as he could throw the lever. Beside him along the length of the saddle. Hat's rifles talked in loud, harsh signals. Echoes of the shots bounced back at him from the flatland below and the ridge was a series of bright-blooming orange flashes spearing forward from the crest of land. Punctuating the ragged, heavy volley were the deeper reports of Latigo's .50-caliber Spencer and Shorty Palumbo's wicked .45-90 Sharps.

The world had erupted into a maelstrom of booming sound and powdersmoke flashes; and down below, the Pitchfork steers began to signal their growing panic to one another. Like a ponderous locomotive, the herd began to move. The two mounted nighthawks were racing along the flanks, trying to head off the leaders, but Sebastian observed with a tight smile that the riders would be too late to stop the full-scale stampede. Farther ahead,

DeSpain's camp had suddenly become the center of abrupt, confused, frightened activity, as men ran to their horses, forsaking bridles, mounted bare-back and ran hatless for their lives before the onrushing herd. The shouts of men's voices rose from the plain and two or three guns opened up briefly down there, but were soon silenced when their owners forgot their anger in the fear of a need to escape.

Sebastian plugged fresh shells into the side gate of the Winchester, threw a new series of shots at the heels of the retreating cattle, and rammed the rifle into its saddle boot. 'All right. Let's go home.'

His voice lifted in high signal, rallying his crew; and then, before they went down the back of the ridge at a gallop, they paused briefly to send a last glance back at the wild confusion below. Pitchfork was running full out, horses and cattle and men. Sebastian saw the vanguard of the herd plow through the campfire, extinguishing it; then he grinned. 'A good night's work. Let's go.'

# CHAPTER EIGHT

With the first blue of dawn he was out of his blankets and at the well shaving. After a quiet breakfast at which every man, though he might have tried to disguise it, showed anxious concern, Sebastian stood before the bunkhouse with loose weariness, a tall and thin-flanked man with a lot on his mind. He moved with a tired swing of his shoulders, and tramped across the veranda to knock at the house door. Oddly, it occurred to him now for the first time that this house at whose door he knocked, was his own house, belonging to him. All this that he surveyed was half his own, if he only had the strength and wits to keep it. It was a strange new feeling, one that would probably take him a long time to get used to. Like all working cattlemen he had long harbored the dream of some day owning his own ranch. But for most like him the day never came; even at foreman's wages a cowhand hardly earned enough to keep himself in clothing and gear.

Looking across the yard, he saw 'Sus, climbing stiffly down the barn roof where he had kept watch all night against the possibility that an enraged Buck DeSpain might make an open attack against Hat. He called across the yard at 'Sus, 'Get some grub and some shut-eye.'

'Sus nodded and trudged into the cook shack. Frowning, Sebastian turned and knocked again at the heavy oak door. His door. It was still an unwelcome realization, a new relationship hard to get used to.

Presently the door swung open and Nora stepped aside to let him enter. Her eyes were tired and when she swept a half-listless hand back along the side of her head, smoothing her hair, he saw the lines of fatigue in her face. She said, 'I was just feeding Ray some broth. Come in, Clay.'

He closed the door gently. 'How is he?'

'Awake. He can't see, though, and he has trouble talking.' She sounded as though the capacity for emotion had been washed out of her by a night of tears.

Sebastian said gently, 'He's lucky he has you, Nora. Stay by him.'

'Don't worry,' she said, and when he thought about it, it was a strange thing for her to be saying to him. He looked at her more closely, and then in her eyes he saw a greater strength than he had thought was there. He was glad of that. She said simply, 'He's my man, Clay.'

'He's a lucky one,' Sebastian answered, and tried to smile for her.

She went across the room to sit wearily in Jesse's big chair. She looked very small against its high, carved back. She said, 'What happened last night, Clay?'

'We stampeded Buck's herd for him. It won't do us much good, but at least it gives us a little time. Anyway, now he knows we weren't bluffing.'

'Neither was he,' she said hollowly, and Sebastian knew she was thinking of what had been done to Queene. 'Clay, no man should be allowed to do that and go on living.'

'I know.' His tone was gentle.

Her voice was almost curt when she said, 'We're going to fight them all the way to the end, Clay. If I have to sacrifice every Hat puncher, I want to pull Buck DeSpain's greed down around his filthy ears and grind his nose in the dirt.'

'You're not thinking straight, Nora,' he said, thinking of what Kelcy had told him yesterday. It was an odd reversal of positions.

Outside, full morning sun had replaced the gray break of dawn, and through the window he saw Lucio walking across the dusty yard, probably to clean the corral and barn, doing his chores as though nothing awry had ever happened in Massacre Basin. That was Lucio, a hard-working hand with stolid loyalty and complete competence to handle his job. Sebastian felt lucky to have such men on his crew; he said again, 'We're not going to sacrifice anybody, Nora. DeSpain can be licked without shoving our boys into the mill.'

'How?'

'I don't know,' he admitted. 'But there's got to be a way.'

'There isn't,' she said flatly. 'All that man will understand is a gun shoved under his nose and a trigger pulled.' Her mouth corners sagged with a display of bitterness unlike anything he had ever seen in her. Always before he had regarded Jesse's daughter as a spoiled brat, a kid happy as long as she had her playthings, her favorite saddler and her pretty clothes and Ray Queene. Now he was seeing, for the first time, a new side of her.

The wash of the force of his thinking seemed to impress her, though he had not spoken. She said, 'Yes, I've changed, Clay. Seeing what that man did to Ray would change anybody—or kill him.'

'You'll be all right,' he said, watching her carefully. He saw the darkness of her expression, the heavy roll of her lips. There was bleakness in her eyes, the shadow of her feelings; and he began to worry deeply. He said, 'Listen, Nora. Don't do anything without thinking it out. Not anything at all.'

'Why,' she said, 'what do you mean?'

He didn't answer; he swung quickly across the room and into the hallway, and into the room where Ray Queene, or what was left of him, lay.

Queene's face was a mass of scabs and black bruises. Both of his eyes were hidden behind swollen flesh and his blond hair, thickened with dark stains of blood, lay matted against his head. The one hand that lay above his blankets was bruised and swollen around the knuckles. When Queene spoke, Sebastian hardly recognized his croaking voice. 'That you, Clay?'

'Right here, partner.' He tried to force joviality into his tone. 'Looks like a horse

95

stomped you.'

'It was a snake,' Queene said. His voice hissed through broken teeth. 'A snake with big boots. Clay, don't do anything rash about Slade. That's just what Buck wants.'

'I know,' Sebastian said. 'What did the doc do to you?'

'Straightened my nose out. Put a corset on me—Slade busted some ribs. He put some salve on my face and told me to leave it unbandaged so the air could clean me.' Queene chuckled deep in his throat. 'I'm a fine specimen of God's handiwork, Clay. What do I look like?'

'You look like hell,' Sebastian told him cheerfully.

'You go to hell,' Queene answered quickly.

'Maybe,' Sebastian said. 'Anything I can get you?'

'Caviar,' Queene said smugly. 'I crave caviar, Clay. I'm tired of beef soup.'

'What in hell is caviar?'

'Sturgeon eggs,' Queene said. 'I had some in San Francisco once at a crummy little Russian café.'

'Yeah,' Sebastian muttered. 'Sure. I'll go catch a sturgeon right away. In Dry Creek maybe.'

'They swim backwards,' Queene mused. 'To keep the dust out of their eyes.'

'Sure,' Sebastian said again. He laid a gentle hand on Queene's shoulder, hesitated a moment, and left the room quickly, yesterday's hot anger rising once again in his chest. He strode straight through the big main room, not even glancing at Nora, and stopped outside on the porch to call across at the corrals, 'Lucio, hitch up the buckboard for me.'

Lucio nodded and disappeared into the barn. Beside him, Nora came out onto the veranda. 'Where are you going?'

'Arrowhead. We're short on grub again.'

'Pick up some more of that salve from the doctor,' she said. 'I used most of it on Ray's face during the night.'

His glance swept her face. 'You stayed up all night with him?'

'Yes,' she confessed.

'Then go in and get some sleep. I'll send Shorty up to the house to watch him '

'All right,' she said wearily, and went inside. Sebastian stopped at the bunkhouse, left orders with Shorty, and went on to the corrals, where he climbed to the buckboard's spring seat and accepted the reins from Lucio.

'Boss.' Lucio's tone was awkward. 'Take care.'

Sebastian smiled. 'Sure.' Then he clucked to the horse and the buckboard pitched forward along the fence line. When he thought back at what Lucio had said, it moved him deeply; that was as close as Lucio had ever come to expressing his feelings for his boss.

Heat pulsed along the ground. Against the

back of his shirt the sun burned like a roaring fire; he pushed his hat forward over his brow and kept watch on the horizons, a care that he realized was quickly becoming habit with him in these days of tension. The wagon rocked over the wide sweeps of land and here and there, in small grass pockets, he saw little bunches of Hat cattle that had drifted home after the storm. When he thought of Buck DeSpain, the dark surface of his rawboned jaw lengthened and he thought, *The only way to end this will be to face DeSpain with nothing between us but smoke.* But DeSpain was a shrewd man and likely it would be almost impossible to find him in a position that gave him the opportunity.

When he was approaching the rim above the Massacre, a horseman rode into sight, milled for a moment with his rifle raised, and wheeled behind a hill. Sebastian frowned and drew his Colt, holding it ready. But he achieved the river without incident and clattered onto the bridge. The steel buttstrap of the revolver was hot against the heel of his palm; he holstered it after a single look backward, and tooled the buckboard past the trees to the barren flatness of Arrowhead. There he set the brake and stepped down at Jackson O'Keefe's store. He gave a further moment's speculative thought to the rifleman he had seen briefly above the river bluff, and then put it from his mind and stepped inside

98

the store's dimness.

Kelcy was not in evidence. From his shirt pocket Sebastian withdrew a penciled list and placed it on the counter top. 'Got all this?'

'I've got it,' O'Keefe said. He seemed nervous. 'But we've got to do cash business from here on out, Clay. Things are getting rough.'

'Aren't they?' Sebastian said gently. He pinned his gaze on O'Keefe. 'Buck DeSpain put you up to this.'

'I didn't say that.' The storekeeper's answer was too quick.

'He's got you scared half out of your pants,' Sebastian said sourly. 'Probably threatened to take all his business to Benson if you gave Hat any credit. Is that it?'

O'Keefe's hands fluttered. 'You're just making wild guesses, Clay.'

'Am I?'

O'Keefe wouldn't meet his eyes. Finally he picked up Sebastian's list and pretended to read it. 'Maybe you haven't heard, Clay. But there's a war brewing on the Massacre and I can't afford to have a bunch of I.O.U.'s around here signed by men that may not live to pay the bill. I'm sorry, but that's the way it is.'

Sebastian shook his head. 'Benson's a two-day ride from here, bucko. DeSpain's bluffing you. Can't you see that?'

Suddenly O'Keefe's eyes flashed. 'Damn it, Clay, Buck DeSpain hasn't bullied me into anything. I run my business the way it's got to be run. So do you. Nobody's bought me and nobody gives me orders. Now get off your high horse.'

Sebastian watched him carefully; abruptly he decided O'Keefe was telling the truth. 'My apologies,' he said. 'I'm jumpin' at shadows. Look, I'll write you out a draft on our bank at Bisbee.'

O'Keefe brightened, glad to end the argument. 'Sure Clay. That'll be fine.'

'Sorry I jumped you,' Sebastian said again. He felt a little foolish. 'Kelcy around?'

'She went to lunch a little while ago. Ought to be back soon. Let's see; you'll find the flour barrels out back in the storeroom. I'll collect the canned goods here for you.'

'Much obliged.' Sebastian turned back to the farther door. Then he paused. 'Got any caviar?'

'What?'

'Never mind.' He went back into the storeroom.

He was just lifting the last of the supplies into the buckboard when Kelcy came along from the café on her brother's arm. Sebastian turned away from the wagon and touched a finger to his hatbrim. Kelcy showed him her easy, warm smile; and Sebastian nodded to Dan McGarrity. McGarrity said, in an idle tone, 'I hear Pitchfork had a little accident last night.'

'That so?' Sebastian said, keeping his glance innocent.

'Somebody stampeded a herd. Scattered eight hundred cows all over the hills back of Arrowhead Flats. Buck DeSpain's just about ready to bust a gut. Says it'll take his crew three days to comb all those cows out of there.' McGarrity chuckled.

Sebastian's brow creased. 'Where'd you hear about this?'

Kelcy spoke up, 'DeSpain's in town, Clay. At Fancy Lee's place.'

'Ah,' Sebastian said softly.

'Hold it, Clay,' Dan McGarrity said quickly. 'Don't do anything you might regret later; don't do anything I'd have to lock you up for. I'd hate to have to do that.'

'Don't worry,' Sebastian said. But his eyes were narrowed with thought.

'All right,' the deputy said uncertainly. He turned and sauntered back the way he had come, looking for all the world like a man with nothing at all on his mind. He knelt at a little weed clump to pull up a long straw and stick it in the corner of his mouth, and disappeared around the corner of the dry-goods store.

Jackson O'Keefe was just coming out the door. He held up a small oval tin. 'Happened to find this tin of caviar, Clay. You still want it?'

Sebastian grinned. 'You bet. Toss it in.'

O'Keefe did so and then, with a single

glance toward Kelcy, instead of returning into the store he walked off in the general direction of Chaffee's bar. Sebastian grinned at the storekeeper's back and took Kelcy's arm. 'He sure thinks he's a sly old buzzard, doesn't he?'

'He's sweet,' Kelcy said. 'I hope nothing happens to him because of this trouble DeSpain is stirring up.'

He followed her inside to take up his habitual seat atop the barrel behind the counter. When the girl sat down he did not speak, but only sat watching her with the gravest of expressions. After a while he could see he had stirred her; it was in the slow parting of her lips, in the steadiness of her glance. There was a deep and faraway glow in her eyes when she said, 'Sometimes I wish we were all a thousand miles from here in some peaceful country. The raw edge hasn't worn off Arizona yet, Clay. We have to fight too much here.'

'It's the fighting that makes the rewards worthwhile,' he said.

'Not if you die in the fight.' Her eyes were wide and round.

He said, 'Why, you're scared, aren't you?'

She nodded sadly. 'I don't want anything to happen to you, Clay. Ever.'

'Nothing ever will,' he said stoutly, and wished he felt as confident as his voice sounded.

Her lips were sweet, turned heavy by the

gentle gravity of her thoughts. He watched the tilt of her face. Her shoulders were delicately square and motionless. Her breasts moved softly with her breathing; her face was expressive but calm now, and proud. Then his lips pulled apart and he laughed softly. 'Now who's taking his trouble to who?'

She matched his laughter. 'I'm sorry, Clay. We have so little time together—we ought to make it count for more, shouldn't we? We ought to have more pleasure.'

'I get all the pleasure I need,' he said quietly, 'just being here.'

She smiled for him, a smile that held many things. She swayed forward and he caught her shoulders and dipped his head. Her lips clung to his mouth. She moved her face, and said, 'I wish it was all over, Clay. I can't help it.'

'It will be,' he answered, and got to his feet. 'When it is over, I want you to marry me.' His tone and his glance were grave.

She came to him, raising her arms to the back of his neck, pressing her body against him, pulling his head down. 'Don't make it too long,' she whispered, and kissed him again.

There was a good, strong feeling in him when he went out into the sun. But then, when he looked over the buckboard at the end of Chaffee's saloon, he saw standing hipshot at the rail Buck DeSpain's big sorrel. Sight of it brought him all the way back down from the heady feeling he had enjoyed so briefly.

103

Making his quick decision, he walked around the end of the wagon, hitched his holster around firmly, and strode forward through the dust. Half across the intervening distance, he changed course and so came up to Fancy Lee's place at the back door. With his hand on the latch he paused, shutting his eyes tightly for a few moments to make them ready for the relative dimness inside. Then he opened the door and stepped boldly inside.

His eyes took the whole scene in with a single sweeping glance. DeSpain, his head turning in surprise, stood at the bar, its only patron. Behind the bar, dressed immaculately according to habit, was Fancy Lee Chaffee, and wisely Chaffee did not move a muscle. Gray and indistinct, someone stood in the far corner of the room, but that man neither moved nor spoke, and so Sebastian put the full weight of his attention on Buck DeSpain's big shape.

DeSpain stood rooted by the bar. Slowly his fat arms rose away from his sides; and when he spoke his tone was calculated. 'I wear no gun, Clay.'

Sebastian felt sudden, cheated rage. 'No,' he said. 'I don't guess you would, Buck. You're too smart.'

'That's right,' DeSpain said easily. 'Come have a drink.'

'Not with you.'

'Easy,' Fancy Lee Chaffee said. 'Take it

easy, Clay.'

There seemed to be something intentionally meaningful in Chaffee's tone, and Sebastian wondered about it. But then he walked slowly forward along the bar until he was within a yard of DeSpain, and halted. DeSpain said, 'We had some trouble last night.'

'Dan McGarrity told me about it.' Sebastian grinned through clenched teeth. 'Two can play at a game, Buck.'

He was thinking of last night, and of Ray Queene's beating—two incidents that could not be traced to their perpetrators; and he knew DeSpain understood his meaning. He said, 'Buck, I want you to understand that everything you do, Hat will throw right back in your teeth.'

DeSpain took on a bored look. 'Is that all you came to tell me?'

Fancy Lee carefully placed a glass of whisky before Sebastian, and Sebastian picked it up and sipped from it. Looking at DeSpain over the rim of the glass, he said, 'You can't get what you want without starting a range war, Buck. Wars are expensive. Every man that dies will be on your conscience. Is that what you want?'

'I've got no conscience,' DeSpain said. His voice droned; and Sebastian thought, *Why, I guess that's so.* It made him feel sick. DeSpain's moon face was heat-swollen and there was a half-wild roundness in his eye; but his voice was precise and hard. 'Whatever a man has he can only keep by being tougher than anybody else, Clay. And a tough man can't afford a conscience. You see?'

'No,' Sebastian said flatly. 'A man who's that tough can't live long. You'll die by the gun, Buck, unless you start thinking about the people you hurt.'

'Only a man who can't take care of himself gets hurt. And if he can't take care of himself, he doesn't worry me. Clay, you'd be smart to sell out to us. The offer still stands. I don't want a fight any more than you do.'

'Then don't start one. I figure we're even now, Buck. Except for Cliff Slade, but I'll take care of him in due time. Call off your dogs now and you'll save all of us—yourself included—a lot of grief.'

DeSpain grinned derisively. Last night's stampede had rubbed his pride; it showed in the drawn tautness around his lips and eyes. His words had a flat ring to them, 'Hat is open range, cowboy. Try and stop me, and you'll be bucking the law.'

'You're dead wrong,' Sebastian said thinly, 'and I tried to save you dying to find it out.'

'Ah,' DeSpain said harshly. 'Sometime this week my herd moves onto Hat. You be somewhere else, cowboy, and nobody will get hurt. Otherwise, folks will remember that it was you, not me, that started the shooting. I'll just be pushing cows.' He grinned again and

106

turned with a quick snap of his burly shoulders, and left.

Not until then did the gray, shadowy man in the far corner come forward; and then Sebastian saw that it was Joe Chess, DeSpain's bantam ramrod, and he understood Fancy Lee Chaffee's earlier warning. Joe Chess said in a wheezing voice, 'You don't know how close you come to it when you walked in that door, bucko.' He turned through the door and disappeared after his boss.

Sebastian turned to the bar and picked up the whisky glass. He raised it in silent toast, which Chaffee acknowledged with a casual nod, and drank.

CHAPTER NINE

The bashful horseman still followed him at a distance, too far to be recognized. Sebastian turned in the saddle to frown over his shoulder at the rider who followed him so patiently. Ever since he had left the buckboard at Hat and ridden out on horseback, he had been aware of the man tailing him; by now that man had become a steady irritant, an itch that Sebastian felt the need to scratch. Presently, in a small hollow of land, he halted and sat long enough to smoke a cigarette through, whereupon he dismounted, drawing his rifle

107

from the saddle boot, and settled against the stony soil with his eyes on the hogback he had just ridden over.

While he waited for the rider to appear, he recognized in himself a strange feeling, as though he had forgotten to do something, and couldn't remember what it was. In half anger, he sent his mind back through the day, bringing scenes forward in order, tying to find the missing piece. After leaving Chaffee's, he had stopped by Noah Teale's to boost the lawyer into working harder on the land grant claim case. Then he had indulged in a bath and shave at the barber-dentist's 'dobe, and afterward he had tooled the buckboard out of Arrowhead. If his quiet pursuer had picked up his trail there, he hadn't noticed it, though he did remember seeing a strange rider on the outskirts of town before he had ridden in.

Soon he heard the ruffled tramp of a horse, and lifted his rifle with tight satisfaction. There was quiet loneliness on the land that touched his senses; a little breeze moved wearily above the ground, suspending wisps of dust. He squinted against the glare, pinning his attention on the point of the hogback where his own back trail came into view. Hoofs sounded louder, and he eared the rifle hammer back silently. Sun on the front sight glanced against his eyes and he moved the rifle barrel.

Finally the pursuing horseman appeared

atop the ridge and put his horse down the near slope. The man rode down half the slope with his head bowed as though deep in thought; then he lifted his glance, and for the first time saw Sebastian, crouched a short distance before him.

Sebastian said, 'Howdy, Rivers.'

A long sigh escaped from Jeremiah Rivers' throat. He tarried briefly where he was, and then put his horse down the intervening distance to halt close beside Sebastian. The gunman said, in a mild tone, 'Good afternoon.' And looked down at Sebastian with an utterly blank face.

'I reckon you made a mistake,' Sebastian said.

'I was careless,' Rivers admitted.

Sebastian stood up slowly, keeping his rifle trained on Rivers. 'How long have you been following me?'

'All day.'

'Any particular reason?'

Rivers allowed a slight smile to touch his lip corners. 'Perhaps. You seem to be headed toward the Monarchs. Might you be looking for Cliff Slade?'

'I might.' Sebastian lifted his thumb off the hammer and lay it alongside the Winchester's sideplate.

'In that case,' Rivers murmured, 'I might just ride along with you.'

'Sure thing. Just unbuckle your guns and

hand them down. Then we'll ride.'

Rivers shook his head. 'I never give up my guns, sir.' His face always seemed sad; perhaps it was the droop of his black mustache, or the hollows under his eyes.

'I guess you don't have much choice,' Sebastian said, gesturing with his rifle. 'Unless you want to try and beat the drop.'

'I probably could beat you,' Rivers said thoughtfully; and Sebastian felt it wasn't just an idle boast. 'But I'd prefer not to,' Rivers said. 'Do you intend to force my hand?'

'No. All I want to do is get you off my back. Hand down your guns, Rivers.'

Rivers shook his head. 'I guess not. It's a matter of principle, sir. I think you'll understand.'

Sebastian felt his belly tightening. He said evenly, 'I'm getting damn tired of your plantation manners, mister. Whatever principles you've got you can make exception to. Now I won't ask it again. Hand them down.'

Rivers' head was still moving back and forth. The buck-skinned gunman had let his reins fall across the pony's withers, and now he sat loose in the saddle, his hat shading his features, looking down and not speaking. He watched Sebastian's eyes, and Sebastian's gun, and finally, after the longest interval, he spoke as though he had just made a distasteful decision.

'I hadn't wished to do this, sir.'

Then Sebastian saw the slight rise of the man's shoulder. Sebastian lifted the rifle muzzle; he heard a click, sharp in the stillness; and he pulled the trigger. The sound of the shot slammed back at him from the hogback. Then he stepped back quickly as Rivers pitched out of the saddle.

The buckskin-clad man hit the ground with the point of his shoulder and rolled to a jarring halt against the base of a heavy boulder. His right-hand gun, the one he had drawn, skidded several feet onto the dust. Sebastian whirled to keep the muzzle of his Winchester trained on Rivers; but when Rivers fell by the rock, he stayed there, not moving. For a moment Sebastian thought he was dead. He let the rifle barrel dip and felt the violent trembling of his own hands. The pound of his own heart was heavy in his chest; for a while he had a drowning sensation, as though he couldn't get enough air into his lungs, no matter how strongly and gustily he breathed.

The white land's shimmering brightness beat against his eyes; his flesh was pallid, even under his deep tan, from the slowly draining fear in him. Then his fists locked hard around the rifle, for Rivers had moved.

The gunfighter's lean face turned slowly toward him and Sebastian saw the tightness of pain drawn across his cheeks. Rivers spoke huskily, 'You made a bad job of that, cowboy.'

'I didn't guess I had time to figure windage,'

Sebastian said, in a slightly sardonic tone.

'You've got fast reactions,' Rivers said. He seemed to be musing to himself more than talking to Sebastian. 'Most men wouldn't have pulled the trigger in time.'

Sebastian shook his head in disagreement. 'You can't beat the drop, Rivers.'

'No?' Rivers' eyes rose; there was a bright point of flame behind them, the flame of pride. 'Take a look at my gun.'

'First I'll take this one,' Sebastian said, and knelt to draw Rivers' left-hand revolver from its tied-down scabbard. Then he turned and picked up the gun that had flown from Rivers' fist.

The breath went out of his chest in a sudden gust. He said, 'It's cocked.'

'That's so,' Rivers said. 'You came that close to it, my friend.'

Sebastian was still watching the gun in his fist. It was a common looking Colt, short-barreled with the metal's blue worn thin around the muzzle and trigger guard and back-strap. The front sight had been filed down. And the heavy, thumb-busting hammer was drawn back to full cock. Amazement was written on Sebastian's features. Rivers had drawn fast enough to get his Colt out of its scabbard, line it up on Sebastian, and pull the hammer back fully—all in the time it took Sebastian to move his rifle a few inches and pull its trigger. Another tenth of a second, he knew, and their positions would have been reversed now—only the loser wouldn't have remained alive.

He let the revolver hammer gently down to safety-cock and knelt by Rivers. 'Let's have a look,' he said matter-of-factly, and began to unbutton Rivers' shirt. He wondered if the gunfighter could feel the tremor in his fingers. Once he caught Rivers' quiet eyes staring up at him; they seemed to be smiling at him.

The heavy .44-40 slug, at a range of only a few feet, had sheared upward along Rivers' chest, glanced off the breast-bone and left at the front of his shoulder. Sebastian went to his horse and brought back his canteen, and began to wash the long, scraping wound. Rivers watched without blinking. Sebastian could see the thin, naked stripe of white along the breastbone where the bullet had ricocheted. Rivers said calmly, 'There's a clean kerchief in my hip pocket.'

Sebastian found the handkerchief and refolded it length-wise to cover the wound. Then he removed his own bandanna and tied it around Rivers' chest, over one shoulder and under the other arm, to hold the bandage in place. He said, 'This isn't the first time you've been hit.'

'Nor the last,' Rivers said cryptically. 'My friend, you might have done yourself better to leave me lie here for the sun and the coyotes.'

'No,' Sebastian said. He tied the bandanna

tight and rebuttoned the buckskin shirt. 'You claim to be a gentleman. If you are, you'll remember I could have left you out here and taken your horse. You'll remember I could have let you bake under this sun while that wound festered. And you'll remember that I didn't.'

'I see,' Rivers said. There was admiration in his eyes. 'So I'll have to remember that I owe you my life.'

'That's it. A gentleman would ride straight out of Massacre Basin and never look back.'

'Well,' Rivers said, with a quizzical turn to his lips, 'I used to consider myself a gentleman. A long time ago.'

'Can you make it to your feet?'

'Give me a hand,' Rivers said. Then, with most of his weight against Sebastian, he moved slowly to his horse and leaned there against the saddle, resting and breathing heavily.

Sebastian left him there momentarily while he went back and scooped up the twin short-barreled Colts. Methodically he punched the cartridges out of them and then, with both guns empty, he slid them into Rivers' holsters.

'I'm obliged,' Rivers murmured. 'Sebastian, if you live long enough, you'll be able to tell your children with some pride that you're the only man alive that ever took Jeremiah Rivers' guns away from him.'

'Come on,' Sebastian grunted, and hoisted the gun-fighter into the saddle. Then he stepped back, swept his hat off his head and mopped sweat from his forehead with his sleeve. 'You'd best stop in Arrowhead to let the doctor treat that wound properly. Then ride on out, Rivers. You owe me that much.'

'You hold the high cards,' Rivers admitted. 'Damn few men I've met that I've been proud to know. You'll do, my friend. *Adios.*' With that, Rivers turned with a small grimace of pain and gigged his pony slowly up his own back trail.

Sebastian watched him go. Only when Rivers had disappeared over the ridge did Sebastian turn, pick up his rifle and canteen, and trudge to his horse. Ahead rose the high timber and stone ramparts of the Monarchs; he turned that way and lifted the pony to a trot. Catclaw and bronze grass grew low along the slopes and the ever-present silver dust raveled high behind him. The open collar of his shirt displayed a triangle of sunburned flesh and his hands, dark and big-knuckled, were scarred and calloused. A close-guarded stiffness held him, the afterwash of shock and he found himself becoming jumpy, listening with acute attention to whatever signals the gently drifting air brought. But he was alone on the wide land, a tall man on horseback riding briskly toward the sharply rising peaks.

His mind lay on Jeremiah Rivers, wondering how any man could live with the certain knowledge that one day he would die by the gun, that his life was measured by the speed of his own hand and the constant awareness of everything that moved within bullet range of him. Every time an ounce of lead nicked him—and there had been many, judging by the scars on his body—he was taking out a new loan. And Rivers had to awaken each morning knowing that this might be the day the loans were called.

The darkly ridged hills grew around him as he advanced. No sound broke through the stillness of this lonely world, and in the last blue of dusk he entered the wide mouth of an ascending canyon, and knew he had achieved the rim of the Monarchs. This was the far edge of No Man's Land and it would be foolhardy to continue into unfamiliar enemy territory at night. So he dismounted in the shelter of a high-sided draw and made dry camp, putting out the horse on short picket and lying down with his saddle for a pillow and his hand resting against his loaded Winchester. This was Lew Kohlmeier's stronghold; Sebastian slept light.

## CHAPTER TEN

In the middle reaches of the Monarchs, the dawn shone clear and cool. By old habit, he lit a cigarette before pulling the spare makings of a trail breakfast from his saddlebags. Then, having eaten, he surveyed the horizons watchfully while he cinched up, mounted, and rode out of the little draw.

The trail lifted him into a rocky pass. High-walled red ridges to either side closed down until he threaded the bottom of a deep gorge, descended past the track of a dry creek, and entered the first scrubby evidence of timber. He turned through a series of canyon loops, climbed steeply to the gorge's head, and soon topped the summit. The game trail then dropped him around sharp-cut switchbacks through a descending spiral of canyons and he crossed a narrow, plush little valley. There was a thinly trickling creek ahead, the beginnings of the snow runoff from higher up, and he halted inside the fringe of timber to survey both banks before putting the horse across. Here he encountered a broader, beaten-down trail with evidence of much heavy traffic, and he pulled away from that, not wanting to take unnecessary chances. A cool current seemed to come out of the trees, warning him, and so he drew the Winchester from its boot and laid it across the pommel before he went up the other side of the creek bank. He felt the touch of the wind against his cheek; it was a cool one and he remembered the norther he had weathered at Rifle Springs. He frowned and said aloud, 'Don't get spooky.'

Then, as he rode forward through the

117

tortuous spires of the Monarchs, he took stock of his situation. Jeremiah Rivers, if he could be trusted to keep his word, had removed his own threat, and that was a piece of luck. So far, young Fletch Diedrich had not acted at all since the night he had bravely withdrawn Slash-D's support of Pitchfork. And from everything Sebastian had been able to learn in Arrowhead, DeSpain would be having his hands full for at least a few days rounding up the widely scattered herd Hat had stampeded. It gave Hat breathing space; it gave Sebastian time to hunt down Cliff Slade. But there had been nothing to change Buck DeSpain's stubborn mind, and Sebastian knew the man wouldn't let Hat get away with any simple trick again. It still narrowed down to one solution. The only way to whip DeSpain would be to catch him alone and armed, and challenge him as one man to one man, to determine who would control Massacre Basin. But the chance of finding DeSpain alone and armed, as Sebastian had learned yesterday morning in Chaffee's saloon, was almost nonexistent.

The one thing, he was sure, that stood solidly on Hat's side was the validity of the Ruiz y Ortega grant. But that was no help right now. Again yesterday, lawyer Teale had warned him that it might take years to get the case heard in Federal court, both because of the court's crowded docket, and the delaying tactics DeSpain was sure to use.

There seemed no clear road ahead.

He cut into another game trail farther along the timbered slopes and rode toward the higher reaches, where he pulled off to sit quietly a moment, breathing the horse while he made his decision and thereupon rode straight north, keeping to hollows and gulches to avoid the skyline. Today's particular mission was clear enough; it was personal and yet it was business, in the sense that DeSpain would soon know that Hat was never willing to let him get away with a thing. That much, Sebastian realized sensibly, was not much more than a thin excuse; DeSpain knew Hat's determination already. But Ray Queene still lay abed, shuddering with attacks of pain; and what had once been a strong body and a handsome face would become, at best, a bent frame and a mass of scars. Somehow it seemed a much filthier, much lower kind of attack than a bullet would have been.

It was, of course, not much more than a hunch that turned him north in the direction of Peacock Gap, a hunch that he would find Slade there. He was counting on the probability that Slade would not be bothering to hide, because if Sebastian's original estimate of DeSpain's plan was right, Slade would be expecting Jeremiah Rivers to pull his chestnuts out of the fire for him. The joker whose whereabouts in the deck Sebastian didn't know was Lew Kohlmeier. Whether

Lew was still across the Basin on Pitchfork, or whether after the stampede he had withdrawn his crew to his headquarters at Peacock Gap, was a question there was no way of answering short of riding into the Gap and seeing for himself.

According to the technical limits of the Ruiz y Ortega grant, Peacock Gap was rightfully a part of Hat. But it was so far back in the Monarchs that Jesse Parrott had never bothered to establish his hold on it; in the ordinary run of Hat's business there were many thousands of acres up here, including the Gap, that were entirely useless to Hat. Once, several years ago, there had been a small gold strike at the Gap, and a tiny shanty town had sprung up before the residents had discovered that the lode was shallow, though high grade. Within months the gold had petered out and now all that was left of the would-be boomtown was a small collection of ramshackle, half-collapsed buildings along the irregular banks of the creek. It had become the headquarters camp for Kohlmeier's crew of night riders, and that was all.

He came to the head of a canyon, crossed the rim and went along the side of a parallel ridge, threading the timber. Above his head was a mat of intertwining treetops, shutting out the sky and glooming the visible world. His horse padded on a deep carpet of pine needles and cones. From there he broke out of the canyon, and turned left to come up from the tidings slope behind the town. He tied his horse beside what had been a tool shack, removed his spurs, hung them on the saddle horn, and took down his rifle. Then he wormed up to the top of the slope to put his glance on the weathered settlement below.

The creek, panned dry of gold, ran a short hundred yards from its origin at a high spring. It disappeared into a field of eroded rocks at the Gap's mouth, and went underground. The rock field made a natural watchdog for Kohlmeier; anyone riding across those boulders—and a man would have to if he was coming in Lew's front door—would create enough clatter to warn everyone in town. That was why Sebastian had chosed the steep slope above the Gap.

The town seemed quiet enough. No one was abroad; only one chimney showed a thin spiral of rising smoke. Carefully, Sebastian descended the face of the slope and, moving from tree to tree, advanced as far as the biggest building in the Gap, which from the smell of it was now in use as a stable. He let himself inside and as soon as he did so, felt his stomach muscles tighten. Racked in stalls along the walls were a good half-dozen horses, and their saddles lay on racks, proving these were not just spare mounts.

Some part of Kohlmeier's crew was here. Advancing down the stable aisle, Sebastian tried to identify the horses, but had no success until, near the mouth of the stable, he found Lew Kohlmeier's dun gelding. A long sigh went out of Sebastian's chest. Unconsciously he hefted the rifle and stepped to the front door, and peered outside with care.

The nooning sun cast short shadows along the ground, but they were all the shadows of trees and shacks. Nobody was out in the town. The cabin from which smoke issued was not far away and, remembering the six horses within the stable, Sebastian walked that way, cat-footed and rifle up. He approached the windowless side of the shack, worked his way silently to the end of the blind wall, and peered around past a window sill at the close front door.

The muted sound of sleepy talk came through the wall, but he couldn't tell how many different voices were joining in the conversation. He removed his hat and peered slantwise through the window's cracked glass.

After a long while looking into the dimness, he made out five men in the single long room. Three sat at a table, playing cards. A fourth man, Lew Kohlmeier, stood tall by a window in the far wall, looking thoughtfully outward. And the last man stood over the battered stove warming coffee in a pot. That was Cliff Slade. The man's hand shook visibly. Waiting was probably getting to him.

Where was the sixth man? It disturbed

Sebastian; he dropped away from the window and spent a full five minutes searching out the shadows. But nothing stirred. The only possible answer he could think of was that the man was standing guard out at the mouth of the Gap.

Just past the wall, not fifteen feet away, stood Slade. He had come too far to hesitate now. Still bothered by the unknown whereabouts of that sixth man, Sebastian made up his mind and ducked under the window sill to get to the door. He used his knee to lift the latch and his foot to kick the door in; both hands were holding the rifle and when he stepped inside he had it ready. 'Stand pat,' he commanded.

The three men at the table moved not an inch. At the far window, Kohlmeier's head turned, and he remained still. And at the stove, Cliff Slade whirled and Sebastian caught the terror in his face. Like a cameo, the scene became frozen, with nothing moving for the longest time until Lew Kohlmeier said, in a mild enough voice, 'I never thought you'd have the gall, Clay.'

'I came for Slade,' Sebastian said. His rifle did not move; it was aimed past the three seated men at a point midway along the wall between Kohlmeier and Slade.

Slade got up his bluster. 'Well, I ain't hidin'.'

'Nice of you,' Sebastian murmured. His eyes watched Slade unblinkingly; but in the corners of his vision he commanded all the others. He said, and watched his words fall against Slade, 'Jeremiah Rivers won't be coming up here today, Slade.'

As though a snake had struck at his boot, Slade jumped back, almost upsetting the stove. As its clatter died Sebastian whipped away from the open doorway and stepped back against the wall beside it; the noise might bring that sixth man, and he didn't care to be targeted in the door. Then Slade said, 'How do you know that?'

'Take my word,' Sebastian said. Then, with seeming carelessness, he let the rifle drop out of his right hand, so that he was left holding it by the barrel, pointed up. He leaned it against the wall beside him and stood with his hands empty, facing Slade across the length of the room. 'You can try,' he said, 'any time.'

He had been gambling on Kohlmeier, and now knew he had guessed right, when Kohlmeier said to the three men at the table, 'Stay put, boys. This is private.'

Slade's eyes were wide. 'There's only one way you could have got Rivers off your trail,' he said, in a tight little voice.

'That's right,' Sebastian drawled. He did not elaborate. If these men thought he had won an even battle against Jeremiah Rivers, the fear of him might give him the edge he could well need.

Slade said, 'Then I ain't drawing.'

'Suit yourself,' Sebastian said. 'I'm going to count three. If you haven't drawn your gun by the time I reach three, you're dead, anyway.'

He was bluffing, and could only hope Slade was too spooked to call his bluff. He said, 'One.'

'Hold it!' Slade screamed. Both hands shot skyward. 'I won't draw—I won't!'

'Then you die cold,' Sebastian said levelly. 'Two.'

A lurching sob broke out of Slade's mouth; his hands dropped and his fingers clawed at his holster and Sebastian waited until the man's gun was up before he pulled his own trigger. The sound of the shot crashed through the little room and on its heels, Slade's answering bullet plowed through the floor; for Slade was already falling, already dead. His burly body hit the rammed-earth floor with a thud.

He looked down at Slade and felt the horror of what he had done; he heard, as though from a distance, Lew Kohlmeier's voice.

'Now you're a killer, Clay. That wasn't self-defense. You prodded him into it and you knew he was so scared he didn't have a chance. How do you feel now, Big Rancher? You still figure there's two cut-and-dried sides to the fence and we're on opposite sides?'

Sebastian didn't answer; he couldn't answer. With his revolver still lifted, he stepped back and regained his rifle. Then he holstered the Colt and brought the rifle forward, uncertain

of his next move. The shots would surely bring
the sixth man on the run; and so thinking, he
flattened his back to the wall and said, 'Your
*compadre* will be coming in shortly, I guess.
Any man that opens his mouth to warn him is
dead. Understood?'

'You got it backwards, Clay,' Kohlmeier said
softly. 'You're the dead man. You just killed
yourself when you pulled that trigger. But I
guess you didn't know it then.' He looked
down at Slade's body and prodded it with his
toe. 'Cliff had it comin' to him, but that don't
change anything.'

'Shut up,' Sebastian said tightly, and
listened for sounds of approaching boots
outside. But he heard nothing. Kohlmeier was
still talking.

'There was a time, Clay, when you and I
could have had a hell of a lot of fun. You and I
would've made a real pair. But you had your
high-flown ideas about right and wrong, and it
put us against each other. Well, what about it
now, cowboy?'

'Shut up, Lew,' he said again. Then, after a
measured interval, he said, 'Where's that sixth
man of yours?'

'Afraid I can't help you there,' Kohlmeier
said. 'It's your hand, Clay. You've got to play
it. All alone.'

*All alone.* It seemed to echo hollowly. His
hands shook; and he felt the black stink of
guilt pawing at his vitals. A week ago he'd

been an honest working cattleman. What was he now? What was he now?

He heard scratching outside; then a voice, 'What's up, Lew?'

Sebastian lifted the rifle, trained it on Kohlmeier's belly; and Kohlmeier, frowning, said, 'It's all right, Sam. Come on in.'

Sebastian nodded and waited while Sam entered the doorway; and then the rifle was in Sam's back and Sebastian was saying, 'If you move, move careful.'

'Ah,' Sam said, and with the calm of experience, stood quite still. Sebastian took a single long sideward step to put himself in the open doorway.

He said, 'If any head sticks out this door while I can see it, I'll blow it off.' Then he whirled, slammed the door, and walked backward across the clearing, rifle and eyes on the door. But Kohlmeier was smart enough to know when to fold his hand and wait for a better deal. The door stayed shut. Sebastian backed into the trees and whirled into the stable, where he went down the line with his clasp knife, severing every saddle's cinch. Then he slipped out the rear door, and sprinted up-canyon toward the ridge, beyond which his own horse was posted.

He achieved the horse without incident. A handful of sullen black clouds were climbing over the close peaks to the east. He turned the horse and rode at a canter into the descending mass of the Monarchs. Like a horseman at his shoulder, death rode beside him. He remembered vividly the open-mouthed shock on Slade's face; and he remembered Lew Kohlmeier's talk. 'You had your high-flown ideas about right and wrong, and it put us against each other. Well, what about it now?'

'Now you're a killer, Clay.'

He shook his head and clenched his fists, and rode on. And so, long after dark, his horse stopped at the gate of the Hat corral and he stepped stiffly down to unsaddle. The clouds were marching forward from the Monarchs and he felt the first light touch of rain when he left the barn and walked wearily toward the bunkhouse. A lamp still glowed within. Before he reached the door, a man with a rifle stepped out of the deeper shadows by the tack shed and said conversationally, 'Miss Nora's been worried.'

'All right,' Sebastian said. He had never heard his own voice sound so lifeless. 'Thanks, Lucio.'

Lucio faded back into the shadows. Sebastian changed his course and went up to the main house, and knocked. My house, he thought dryly. The killer's house.

It was a bleak and dismal night. When Nora opened the door he stepped inside and shut it behind him; and as the light changed behind her eyes he guessed that it was all written on his face to see. Nora said, 'You found Slade.'

It was no more than that. He said, 'Yes.'

'I knew it would do this to you,' she said simply. 'But I didn't know how to stop you.'

'You didn't want to stop me,' he said, not really caring.

'No,' she said. 'I suppose that's true. I keep looking at Ray. But I wish someone else had done it. Not you.'

He grunted and sat down wearily in the big chair. Nora said again, 'I knew it would do this to you.'

'You're wiser than I thought.' He said, 'Slade never had a chance. We both knew it before he drew.'

'Neither did Ray,' she said.

'But Ray's not dead.'

'Sometimes I think he wishes he was. He'll never use his left arm. Slade stamped everything out.'

'Yes,' he said, and found more meaning in that than she had intended.

She said, 'You'll get over it, Clay. Keep remembering that.'

'Maybe,' he said doubtfully.

She said, 'I guess you had better know this now, Clay. DeSpain pushed a herd onto Hat today.'

His face rose. 'What? Where did he get the cows?'

'From Diedrich.'

He looked down at his hands. Nora said, 'I don't know whether he took them at gunpoint or Diedrich gave them to him. There aren't any Slash-D people with the herd. But DeSpain knew you were up in the hills and he didn't want to waste time gathering his own herd. Now he's on Hat, and he means to stay.'

Sebastian tried to concentrate on it, but somehow he just didn't care. All he wanted to do was throw over the whole thing and ride a thousand miles from the guilt in his belly. But when he looked up at Nora he knew he had to care. He said, 'How many men are holding the herd?'

'Only three or four. I think DeSpain wants us to make a move against them. That way he'll have a legal lever against us.'

Where would it end? He stood up. 'Well, those cows will keep overnight. I've got to think on it.' He stepped outside into the increasing rain and, not heeding the dampness, walked slowly across the yard. Behind him he heard Nora gently shut the door. Lucio spoke from the dark by the tackshed, 'DeSpain's on Hat.'

'I know.' He went on without pausing, entered the bunkhouse and went past sleeping shapes to his bunk, where he stretched out fully clothed atop the blanket and tried to outrun the bitterness in him. But half a night's flight didn't help; he rolled around on the bunk and felt a huge weight in the pit of his stomach. Past midnight he rose, clapped on his hat and slicker, and sloshed through the flowing yard to the barn, where he saddled a fresh horse and rode off through the rain toward Arrowhead, toward Kelcy McGarrity.


# CHAPTER ELEVEN

He rode through manzanita and scrub oak thickets half drowned by the drizzle, dipped toward Parrott Creek and splashed across the double loop. Not for a long time had he seen such a dreary night; its black was complete. He had to trust the horse to find its footing. Over his right shoulder, somewhere above the Monarchs, a jagged twig of lightning split the sky and short moments later the thunder crashed against his ears. Water coursed down his legs, soaking through his trousers and filling his boots; it runneled down the channels of his broad hatbrim and leaked uncomfortably under the rim of the oilskin poncho he wore. Half an hour out from Hat, with the first hot rush of impatience wearing off, he began to regret choosing such a night for a fool's errand.

Kelcy had her own life and her own problems. He realized he had no right to saddle her with all his own fears and guilt. There was no point in upsetting her any more; and so he changed his mind and was about to swap directions and head home when, for the first time tonight, something Nora had said registered in his mind. 'I don't know whether De-Spain took the Slash-D cattle at gunpoint or Diedrich gave them to him.' This put two ideas in his head and he continued westward to satisfy the first one.

The quickening boom of thunder was the only sound louder than the rain's steady drum. He rode forward, his face squinted ahead in a semi-expectation of trouble. He knew what Kelcy would say. She would say Slade deserved what he got; she would say, as Nora had said that it was a pity Sebastian had to be the one to do it, but someone had to; and it was more his responsibility than anyone else's. She would say there were many ways of looking at a thing, and that instead of putting all his attention on his own guilt feelings he would have to see that a man had to fight or quit, that Hat stood or fell as Sebastian stood or fell, that his avenging Slade's attack on Queene was an accepted tradition of the land and the times in which he lived, though they might be tragic and disagreeable. He knew she would say those things; and he knew she would be right. A man could not compromise with his own principles of right and wrong, despite anything Lew Kohlmeier or any other outlaw might say.

And so, in this way, and even though she was miles away from him, he found himself again leaning on Kelcy's strength, and borrowing of her intelligence. The image of her, lithe and supple, floated before his eyes, strong, clear features crowned with a mass of thick red hair.

Hard metal grated against his ankle, and he reached down into the top of his boot to adjust the position of the little derringer he had taken off the body of Kohlmeier's man McCann, last week out in the Breaks where the Indians had shot him. Lightning flashing on the plain behind him and the rattle of thunder reverberated across the Basin.

At three o'clock he achieved the western boundary of Hat without having seen a single Slash-D cow, and he cursed mildly for not having asked Nora where DeSpain had moved the cattle.

This common boundary with Slash-D ran south from Parrott Creek clear past the western end of Nine-Mile Flats. There was only one thing to do now: cruise the length of that boundary, hoping to find the Slash-D herd. When the thunder rolled again he observed that tonight's weather might prove a great friend to him; and as the thought grew in his mind, a tight grin spread his lips thin. It would make Buck DeSpain look like a fool if the same trick could be pulled on him twice in a row. Sebastian thought, I'd like to see his face.

In the distance, as he topped a hogback, he raised the lights of Slash-D, yellow pinpoints

133

glistening across the dark. It made him wonder what Diedrich was doing awake at this hour, but instead of turning that way, he continued southward along the boundary. Rain poured steadily down on him; he had been soaked through hours before and by now was beginning to feel waterlogged.

It was half an hour before dawn; his face took on a worried frown. If he couldn't find the cattle before daybreak, his plan was no good. It wouldn't suit his purpose to be recognized in daylight. But then, still under full dark, he broke out of a stand of cottonwoods just as a long stripe of jagged lightning illuminated the shallow bowl of ground before him. This was Peyote Wells, at the northwestern tip of Nine-Mile Flats; and this was where DeSpain had put the Slash-D herd. The lightning sharply showed half a thousand steers milling nervously in the bowl, owl-eyed and frightened by the savage sky. Sebastian spoke aloud, 'One good scare and they'll spook halfway to California.' He grinned a high, reckless grin and waited where he was for another lightning flash; and when it came, he spotted the lean-to of the holding crew, high on the opposite slope with two horses ground-hitched near the trees. The other two men rode gently around the perimeter of the herd, trying to keep the steers calm.

Sebastian talked again, 'Buck's getting

smarter. Up on the hill, that camp's out of the line of fire if the cows stampede. And he probably figured a man could run a herd far from water, and there's water right here. But he didn't count on this spooky lightning.' He brought his arms out from beneath the slicker and lifted his rifle. 'Try again, Buck.'

He spurred the horse and ran forward, cutting across the east end of the herd; and as he approached the cattle, he began firing a rapid skyward volley. He ran the length of the herd, whooping high rebel yells, paused to reload, and whirled back along the end of the herd. In the rising bellow of frightened cattle voices he heard the beginnings of the drum of the stampede. Far across the herd, at two corners, the night guards came in view under a quick lightning burst, and Sebastian saw that instead of trying to stay the herd, they were both fanning wide and coming in his direction, rifles raised. DeSpain was through playing games; that much was plain. These men were under orders to let the herd go, but down the man that tried to run it.

But the damage was already done; the herd, milling in a slow circle the moment before, was lined out now; and with a single subsequent crash of thunder, they were on the run, tumbling west toward Slash-D. Laughing softly, Sebastian faded back into the trees from which he had come, and reined in to wait for another look at the two riders pursuing him.

When the lightning revealed the two horsemen, they were riding at a dead gallop to the northeast, toward Hat headquarters. They passed Sebastian's place of concealment by a wide margin and ran on into the wet night. 'Good luck, boys,' Sebastian murmured, and chuckled.

Then he froze. The voice behind him said, 'Put them up, Clay. High.'

Sebastian's face went blank. He thought, *I should have known it wouldn't be that easy.* He said, 'That you, Joe?'

'That's right,' Joe Chess said. 'Don't move, now. I reckon you've had your fun for tonight.'

The little Pitchfork foreman rode out from cover and circled around before Sebastian. Chess held a rifle trained on him and even though he was only a few feet away, Sebastian couldn't see his expression. Chess said, 'Drop the rifle.'

Sebastian opened his hand and let the Winchester fall. Then Chess commanded, 'Now unbuckle your gunbelt. Slow.'

He did so, and let it drop. He felt tightness in his throat. Joe Chess said, 'I guess you been caught red-handed runnin' off Slash-D cows. That don't set too well, Clay.'

'What now?' Sebastian kept his tone even.

'Why, I reckon we'll just ride over to Pitchfork. Then maybe we'll take you in to the deputy.'

'Ah,' Sebastian said softly. 'But I'll never

136

make it to Arrowhead, Joe. I'll be shot in the back—and the way you and Buck will tell it, I was shot trying to escape. Is that it?'

Sebastian moved his horse out of the trees. All the time he felt the tight pressure of Chess' rifle barrel trained on his back; but then, confident and smiling without humor, Chess moved up alongside and kept pace with him, watching him with a wicked, level glance. Then a thought occurred to Sebastian. His right side was away from Chess, concealed from the man. Sebastian lifted his right foot out of the stirrup and raised it so that he could reach into his boot without bending over; slowly his fingers extracted the little derringer he had taken from McCann. With his hand gripped around its tiny butt, he had a moment's hesitation, wondering if the rain had gotten to the powder inside the cartridge. But he had to take that chance; it was his only one.

The first break of dawn was gray and bleak in the east. Chess was riding relaxed beside him, rifle held idly in one hand, as they approached the banks of the Massacre. The rain had diminished to a slight drizzle. Chess said dryly, 'Good weather for our grass.'

'Sure.' Sebastian said, and lifted his hand with the pocket gun. 'Now it's your turn to drop the rifle, Joe.'

Chess's mouth dropped open. He let the rifle go and halted his horse on the bank of the river. There was white water on the Massacre;

the river lapped hungrily, high at the banks, swollen from the night's heavy rainfall and the melting snows flowing into the peaks into its headwaters in the Monarchs. Joe Chess said, 'Well, I'll be damned.'

'I wouldn't doubt that for a minute,' Sebastian told him. 'Now reach around with your left hand and give me your belt gun.'

Chess moved carefully to comply, and handing Sebastian the revolver. Sebastian nodded toward the rushing river. 'You first, Joe.'

'Where are we going?' Chess still seemed flustered at the tables turning so quickly.

'First to Slash-D. I want to show Diedrich that Pitchork isn't God and he doesn't have to lick your boots. Then you can run back to Buck and take him a message.'

'What message?'

'Next time Buck DeSpain or any other Pitchfork man sets foot on Hat, he'll be shot without warning. Hat's putting up No-Trespassing signs as of today.'

Chess laughed. 'You'll never make it stick, Clay.'

'Try me,' Sebastian said. 'Now move.'

His face sullen, Chess swung forward and put his horse down the muddy bank into the Massacre. Chess moved forward and Sebastian hesitated a moment before going into the swift water. Chess was in up to his hips, the horse completely submerged but for its head and floating tail and saddle. Then, when his glance roved upstream, Sebastian lifted his head. A heavy cottonwood, uprooted from the bank somewhere above, was rushing along atop, the water, headed for Chess with mighty velocity. Sebastian shouted, 'Joe—Joe! Turn back!'

But the roar of the river was too loud; his words were swept away downstream. Cursing, Sebastian spurred his horse hard, leaping it into the river. But before he had made his move he saw he was going to be too late. The river churned around him; and out in midstream, Joe Chess' hat-brim turned and his arms flew up. Faintly Sebastian heard the man's high scream of terror when he saw the great log hurtling toward him. Chess brought his arms up before his face and he was bringing his legs up, trying to spring clear of the horse, when the log struck him, smashed him away from his pony, knocked the horse under and plowed on relentlessly.

Spurring madly, Sebastian whirled his horse out of the river and ran along the bank, uncoiling his saddle rope. He passed the front of the onrushing tree and hauled up savagely; but when he looked at the face of the log, Chess was not there. Sebastian turned the horse upstream and ran back, searching for the floating shape. Up above, Chess's horse bobbed up, found footing on a gravel bar, and heaved out of the water on the opposite bank.

Then, more than halfway across the torrent,

he spotted Chess's body tossing limply in the foam. Shaking out a long loop in his rope, Sebastian whirled it above his head and let fly, hoping Chess had enough consciousness left to grab the loop. But the rope was soggy and heavy with water and fell far short. Grimly, he hauled it in and tried another cast. The rope sailed out this time, falling across the Pitchfork man; but the bantam figure did not move and just them Sebastian saw one hand flutter above the water; and Joe Chess went under. Sebastian put his horse into the river, splashing forward as fast as the animal would go; but when he reached the point where he had last seen Chess, there was no sign of the little man anywhere.

He spent a full ten minutes searching the river, then went out, rode down the bank a quarter mile on one side, splashed across, and rode up the east bank to the point where Chess had originally ridden into the Massacre. But it was no use; Joe Chess was gone. Exhausted and soaked, Sebastian stepped down and squatted on the mud bank, his eyes travelling the visible length of the river. But there was only white foam and brown eddies.

Presently he shook his head, mounted wearily, and headed back toward Peyote Wells to retrieve his rifle and gun belt.

*Because of me*, he thought, *four men have died and maybe there'll be more. I should have sold out to DeSpain.* Long ago, he felt, the security that had comforted his plans had been blasted into a thousand fragments; and now men died and other men plotted to kill, and the world was caving in. His own uncertainty colored all his thoughts; and as he rode through the brightening morning, his face was dark.

Dull anger had settled over his cheeks by the time he entered Fletch Diedrich's yard at nine o'clock. His call sang out and he waited before the house without dismounting, casting a glance by habit across the rusty disrepair of tools around the yard, the flaking roofs of barns and outbuildings. Diedrich's crew were all young and wild and none of them had sense enough to keep the headquarters shipshape.

Diedrich came out of the house wearing his Colt; Sebastian said immediately, 'I guess you know why I'm here.'

Diedrich answered quickly. 'I didn't give him those cattle, Clay.'

'Then swear out a warrant. Charge him with rustling.'

Diedrich looked at his toes. His hands moved uncertainly. 'What good would it do to send Dan MeGarrity out there and get him all shot up? DeSpain wouldn't submit to arrest.'

'He wouldn't shoot a lawman,' Sebastian said. 'Give him credit for that much sense.'

Diedrich shook his head. 'You don't know Buck. He's crazy mad.'

Sebastian's lips tightened. 'He's going to be

madder.' Diedrich looked up. 'How's that?'

'Joe Chess drowned in the Massacre this morning. And your herd's back on Slash-D grass.'

'Joe Chess?' Diedrich spoke abstractedly.

Sebastian's response was dry. 'I guess that proves to you that DeSpain and company aren't immortal, Fletch.'

Flushed with anger, Diedrich took a step forward. 'Damn it, Clay, I may be yellow, but don't rub it in. I got to live with myself. How do you figure I felt the other day when Buck just sauntered in, nice as you please, and mentioned he was borrowing some of my cows? You think I liked standing there and taking that from him?'

'You didn't have to just stand there,' Sebastian suggested quietly.

'What else could I do? Listen, me and my crew are keeping out of this whole mess. That's what you wanted and that's what I'm doing. Now, damn it, leave me alone.' Diedrich's eyes were moist; his lips were clenched and he swung back roughly into the house.

With a dissatisfied frown, Sebastian was about to lift his reins when Leila came out into the sun and touched his arm, looking up at him with a plea in her eyes. Sebastian met her glance, not speaking; and she said, 'Try not to be too hard on him, Clay. He may not be everything you want him to be but you can't change the way a man is built. Try to see our side of this; we can see yours.'

He answered with crude bluntness, 'A man can get pretty lame from sitting on the fence too long, Leila. I just don't want him to fall off on the wrong side.'

'Then don't push him,' she said quickly. 'I know he's headstrong, but he really likes you, and he hates DeSpain as much as you do. We all can't be warriors, Clay.'

'All right,' he said. 'Take care of him, then.' His hands rose and he wheeled out of the yard, heading north.

By noon, when he first raised Arrowhead, he was beginning to feel deeply the effects of twenty-four hours in the saddle without sleep. His eyes idly roamed the horizon and then he descended to the town, riding directly to the shabby building that housed the sheriff's office.

Dan McGarrity met him in the door. 'Where you been, Clay?'

'Prowling,' he answered.

McGarrity turned inside and waited for him to follow. The deputy said, 'You look like a man with something on his mind.'

'I want to post a notice,' Sebastian said. 'No trespassing on Hat, effective today. Violators will be shot. Think you can get that clear to Buck DeSpain?'

Breath whistled through McGarrity's teeth. 'That's a little raw, Clay.'

143

'I didn't start this feud,' Sebastian said, 'but by now I'm sick of waiting for DeSpain to move before I defend myself.'

'You may be up for a murder charge if you try and make that stick,' McGarrity said. 'You can't prohibit trespassing on what you don't own. And right now you can't prove you own Hat.'

'And nobody can prove I don't own it,' Sebastian said. 'You're too good-natured for this job, Dan.'

'I'm tough enough when I have to be,' McGarrity disagreed. 'I just don't like to be.'

'Nobody does,' Sebastian said. 'Be sure Buck gets the word.' Without further word, he swung outside to his horse and led it to the stable. There was no point in riding back to Hat just now; he was dead tired and needed sleep. He walked across the muddy ground to Chaffee's saloon and let himself in, and nodded to Fancy Lee, who was the only occupant of the room. Sebastian said, 'I need the use of your bed for a few hours.'

'Help yourself,' Chaffee said incuriously, and went back to his solitaire.

Sebastian entered the dim little cubicle that was Chaffee's home. Removing his muddy boots, he lay back on the bunk and closed his eyes. Just before he fell asleep his mind conjured up an image of four men walking in somber file past him: the Indian, Montez, Cliff Slade, and Joe Chess, bantam cocky and mean. The shadow of McCann, another man dead in Massacre Basin, followed the others; and Sebastian wondered if it would ever end.

Late in the afternoon he rolled upright, scraped the caked mud off his boots and put them on. Then he opened the side door and used a straw broom to sweep the mud out into the dirt. When he entered the front of the saloon Chaffee sat at a table with two plates of food before him. Chaffee said, 'I heard you rustlin' around in there. Thought you might like a bite to eat.'

'Obliged,' Sebastian said, and sat at the table.

'That's all right,' Chaffee said, and smiled. 'It will cost you four bits.'

When he was half through the meal, he looked up to see Dan McGarrity striding in with a purposeful look in his eye. McGarrity said, 'I rode out to Pitchfork to deliver your message. It made Buck pretty mad. But then a couple Pitchfork hands rode in from Peyote Wells. They said somebody stampeded the herd back onto Slash-D last night, and then this noon they found Joe Chess's body washed up on the bank of the Massacre. Buck put two and two together and came out hoppin' mad. When I left he was saddling up his whole crew and sending a man out after Kohlmeier. They mean to hunt you down and kill you, Clay.'

Chaffee looked up at the deputy. 'Couldn't you stop them?'

'They've broken no law,' McGarrity said sourly.

Chaffee said, 'Put DeSpain under bond to keep the peace.' Sebastian told him, 'That wouldn't help. Even if he kept the bond, there are a dozen other men trying to ride me down. And if you put them all under bond, it still leaves Kohlmeier's toughs. No, this is beyond the law now. It's between Buck and me.'

'That's it,' McGarrity agreed. His eyes were sad. 'I wish I could do something, Clay. But my hands are tied.'

'I know,' Sebastian said. 'It's all right, Dan.' He stood up and headed for the door. 'DeSpain probably thinks I'm back on Hat. I've got to get out there in time to keep him from starting a war with my whole crew.'

McGarrity sprang up and grabbed his shoulder, halting him. 'Wait a minute. If he thinks you're out there, don't walk right into it, Clay. When he finds out you're not there, he'll let the others be. Buck doesn't care about Hat any more. I think he's gone clean crazy. All he wants is to nail your hide to the wall—he doesn't care about the others.'

'But he may hurt them as a way of getting at me. He's already done that once, with Ray Queene. You stay put here, Dan. I won't walk into anything.' He nodded to Chaffee and stooped to go out the door.

By the time he saddled his horse and rode away from Arrowhead at a canter, the sun was

146

far west in the sky and he knew there was only an hour's light left. He gigged the pony and rattled across the wooden bridge over the Massacre, wondering what wire had torn loose in Buck DeSpain's mind. DeSpain must know that even though McGarrity couldn't touch him now, the law would surely bring him down if he killed a man so brazenly. Yet DeSpain was rushing headlong into that kind of trap, a trap of his own making. Of course, Sebastian thought, it was little consolation to know the man would be brought to justice for his murder. The thing to do now was stop DeSpain from hurting anyone else—stop the man any way he could.

When he topped the rise above the juncture of Parrott Creek and the Hat-Slash-D line, he stopped to breathe the weary horse and survey the land ahead. No riders showed; and he felt a little better about that. Perhaps after all DeSpain wasn't headed directly for Hat; or perhaps he was awaiting Kohlmeier's reinforcements.

As he looked out over the rolling leagues of grass, he felt a sudden fierce pride in these vast acres. This was his land, a land he had helped the old man carve out of the wilderness. No one had the right to take it from him. He looked across the width of the Basin at the towering chain that was the Monarchs, and thought, *You've stepped one foot too for, Buck.*

The shot rang out with startling abruptness.

He felt his body jar in the saddle with brute shock; he whipped his head around, not yet feeling pain, and raised his rifle instinctively as a second shot winged past. His eye found the rifleman then, a burly rider on a paint pony two ridges away; and he lifted his Winchester and pumped three shots that way. With some satisfaction he saw that rider fling up his arms, heard his faint cry, and saw the man gallop away, bent over the saddle with pain.

But then the rifle slipped from Sebastian's fingers. He tried to grip the saddle horn; his head spun and he grinned a silly grin and slid unconscious out of the saddle.


## CHAPTER TWELVE

He came awake painfully. There was a knife in his side; there were points of light whirling in his head, keeping him dizzy. His eyes fluttered open; he felt a wave of pain roll through him; he shut his eyes again. After a while the pain seemed to subside and he looked around. It was dusk, the sky graying fast. He lay against the bole of a mesquite on a slope, several yards below the trail. His gun lay beside him where it must have fallen; he reached for it slowly, retrieved it, and slid it down into the holster. Then his eyes shut involuntarily as the knife jabbed his side again.

148

Blood was sticky on his shirt, darkening as it dried. He pulled the shirt gingerly out of his pants, grimacing as it ripped away half-scabbed pieces of blood, and looked down at his side. An angry hole gaped below the breastbone, red-rimmed and pulsing. He stirred; a sharp pain tingled up his back and left him weak.

He gave himself a minute to gather strength. The hole was fairly clean, going in the front and out through his back. When he moved he felt no bones cut, and guessed the bullet had passed between ribs. He glanced at the darkening sky. He didn't know how seriously he had injured his ambusher, but if the man had been able to ride as far as Pitchfork, he could expect a party from there within another two hours. He had to get out of here.

He braced his hand against the tree and pushed himself to a sitting position, carefully putting his back to the bole. He couldn't yet bring himself to stand upright. Every motion brought new lances of pain into him and by the time he was sitting up, his jaw was locked and tears slid down his dust-caked cheeks. He had never felt such intense pain. It was impossible to move again without first resting; he gave himself ten minutes, then put his hands against the ground and crawled slowly up the slope on hands and knees. It was about twelve yards. He had to stop seven times and lie flat to regain power enough to go on.

It took him half an hour to reach the trail. His roan stood patiently still, nuzzling through the weeds for grass. The reins dangled; he was thankful the horse had been trained to stand ground-hitched. But it was a hundred feet distant; stubbornly he started crawling.

Within a few yards he caved in. He lay on his side, panting, his head on the earth and his fists clenched to combat weakness and the knives. Night had come but the moon was up in the east. He got to his knees with a terrible effort and began the painful crawl toward the horse; and knew, after traversing two yards that this would never do. It would take all night this way, and he might pass out soon. He made it to a scrub tree and stoically ignored the pain coursing through him while he hoisted himself doggedly to his feet, using the tree for leverage. He looked at the horse, aimed for it, and stumbled forward. Every step jarred him; every step convinced him he could not take another; and every step brought him a few inches closer.

Finally he stood against the horse, his fists locked to the saddle horn and his eyes blinded with salt and water. Lucio—thank God, Lucio knew how to train a horse!

The bullet hole in his back was still oozing blood. He felt it trickle down his back, warm, sticky. He had to stop it up. The knot in his neckerchief was much harder than he'd remembered tying it, but finally he got it free.

He crumpled it into a ball and reached behind him to press the cloth against the wound. He took off his belt and lifted it to bind the bandage in place. As a further thought he struggled his penknife out of his pocket, cut off a corner of his shirt, and bundled it under the belt at the hole below his breast.

Though all these motions had been slow, they had sapped him; and when the horse took a single step forward to follow the grass, he almost toppled. Presently he lifted his foot slowly to the stirrup. He patted the roan's neck; he whispered, 'Steady, steady,' and gripped the saddle horn tight. If the horse moved now he was done. He got the right rein and draped it across the roan's withers, did the same with the left, grasped the cantle with his right hand and bunched all his muscles.

It was excruciating. But he discovered he was lying across the saddle on his belly. The wound throbbed and he knew he was putting too much pressure on it, but he hadn't the strength to move again.

After a great interval he swung his right leg over the horse's hips. He fell forward, catching himself with his hands at the withers, got the reins and kicked the roan's belly.

The horse lurched off down the trail at a jog that jarred him at every step from hair roots to toenails. His knuckles whitened around the horn. He felt blood leaking out under the neckerchief wadded at his back. He swore. He had to keep awake in the saddle; but the continual jarring pain knocked him around in pinwheeling circles and brought down inexorable blackness.

He was still closer to Arrowhead than to Hat and so he had aimed the horse that way, hoping it would keep to the trail. He dozed fitfully in the saddle, awakening every so often when the roan stopped. The minutes passed thus, one hazy lifetime, and with time going by, the numbness of initial shock wore off, and the pain became a sharper stinging rising through his nerves. He welcomed blacking out.

When he next awoke the roan was standing uncertainly before the wooden bridge on the Massacre. The river gurgled by below. The horse moved across the bridge and Sebastian fought to keep his eyes open until the roan had gone as far as a lighted cabin, McGarrity's. He wondered why he was having such trouble seeing it clearly.

It took some effort to unlock his fists from the saddlehorn. He croaked, 'Anybody home?' He was out again before he fell from the saddle; he never felt himself strike the ground . . .

'I never saw a man with such a talent for trouble.' It was a faint voice, a man's voice; and when he finally became able to see through the red fog that clouded his eyes, he found the doctor bending over him. He seemed to be in a bed. He tried to speak but

152

only a guttural sound came out of his throat. The doctor looked up and pushed his head back flat; he said, 'This is the second one of these I've treated tonight. Make you feel any better to know there's a Pitchfork hand in just as bad shape as you are?'

Sebastian tried to lift his hand. He forced words to his lips, 'Doc, if anybody asks, you haven't seen me.'

'I haven't seen you,' the doctor said simply, and stood up. 'You'll be all right after a few weeks in bed and a few more weeks' rest. Though God knows how you'll ever get it around here. I'll be back tomorrow, if I can sneak in. No doubt DeSpain will have the town ringed by then.'

'Thanks, Doc,' he whispered hoarsely. Then another shape took the doctor's place in his vision and he said, 'Hello, Kelcy.'

She didn't speak; he could see she was close to tears. His lips were stretched tight and the angles of his jaw stood out sharply against his skin. He covered his forehead with his own hand and felt it hot; fever was coming on him. He said urgently, 'Don't let them find me, Kelcy.'

She stroked his hair gently and he saw the depth of her eyes. She brushed her lips to his and stood straight. 'I won't.' Her face was at once troubled and caring and loving him; she was like that when a knock sounded on the door. Her eyes flashed around and it was then that Sebastian first realized he was in Kelcy's own room. The girl crossed the room and picked up a rifle she must have just put there. She levered a shell into the chamber and opened the door carefully.

'Don't shoot,' Dan McGarrity said, 'before you see the whites of their eyes. Ain't that the doc I just saw leaving?'

'Clay's hurt, Ben.'

'What? How?'

'Come in.' She set the rifle down and led her brother into the bedroom. McGarrity looked down at him.

'What happened?'

'Gunshot,' Sebastian croaked.

'Who did it?'

Kelcy said, 'I didn't have to ask. Do you?'

'I guess not,' McGarrity said. 'It sort of narrows down to Pitchfork. Clay you can't stay here. Suppose DeSpain goes back to check on your corpse? He will, you can bet. When you turn up missing Buck will start a hunt. He'll turn all his dogs loose and they'll nose over every pebble from here to the Monarchs. This will be one of the first places he'll look.'

'I can't help that,' Kelcy said to him. 'We can't move him when he's like this.'

'What choice have we got?'

'We can gamble.' Their voices faded in Sebastian's consciousness and he felt himself drifting off . . .

He floated between sleep and consciousness

154

then, not able to tell whether the intervals that passed were hours or days. On Kelcy's bed, he turned in high fever, his face reflecting the pain and the cold bitterness in him. Once Kelcy tipped his head up and spooned broth into his mouth but he swallowed little of it.

Then one morning he awoke with his head clear and the knowledge that the fever had broken. He turned his face and said, 'What day is it?'

'Thursday,' Dan McGarrity said. 'Your bullet hole's on the mend.'

*I was shot Saturday,* he thought. 'Where's DeSpain been?'

His question brought no answer; his glance shifted from the deputy's reluctant face to Kelcy. Her eyes were tired; she shook her head and bent forward to touch a palm to his forehead. 'The fever's gone,' she said, and smiled gently. He saw both solemnity and sweetness in her look.

Intimations of their secrets colored his thoughts and he said again, more urgently, 'Where's DeSpain been?'

McGarrity said quickly, 'I haven't seen him since the day you were shot.'

'But you've heard something,' Sebastian guessed. 'Come on, Dan!'

McGarrity's eyes fell. 'He's taken Hat.'

Sebastian thought about it for a minute. 'What do you mean, taken it?'

'Just that. Moved his whole crew and five

thousand cattle onto Hat. He's got men and cows scattered from Dragoon Springs to Peyote Wells and everywhere in between.' McGarrity paused then, shaking his head, and added softly, 'I guess you'll never get him off Hat now.'

Sebastian said, 'What about Nora and my crew?'

'For some reason, DeSpain hasn't touched any of them. He hasn't gone near the buildings at all. Maybe he's getting smarter.'

'Maybe,' Sebastian said. 'But my guess is it was Kohlmeier's common sense that held him back.'

Kelcy had left the room shortly before, and now returned with a platter of food, which she set on the chair while she propped Sebastian up with pillows. 'Think you can handle this?'

'That and another one like it,' he said, feeling the sharp edge of hunger. As he ate he applied his mind to the corner he was boxed into; and after a while such thinking brought a furrowed scowl to his features. He said, 'What I don't understand is why DeSpain didn't send his whole crew out to hunt me down.'

'Because of your funeral,' McGarrity said.

'What?'

'We buried you day before yesterday,' McGarrity said, and grinned at him. 'It was a very touching ceremony. Even DeSpain took his hat off. We told him you'd come crawling into town late that night, after you'd been shot,

156

and had fallen dead out of the saddle.'

'How many people know I'm not dead?' In his characteristic way, Sebastina absorbed this new turn quickly and immediately began to explore its possibilities.

'Just the three of us, the doctor, and Nora. I had to let her in on it. And I suspect she probably told Queene and maybe even your crew—but I'd trust them all the way.'

Sebastian nodded, and immediately regretted that action; it sent new slivers of pain through him. He said, 'Then that explains why Buck didn't move in on Nora. He'll be figuring that with me dead, she'll wear down and quit pretty soon.'

Kelcy removed the empty plate from his lap. 'Get some sleep now,' she whispered, and brushed his lips with hers.

He wondered if they would be able to keep the secret of his being alive long enough for him to get on his feet.


## CHAPTER THIRTEEN

The secret was out; he was almost sure of it. Kelcy had been in O'Keefe's store, talking about him to the doctor, when a man had stepped forward from the rear shadows, his face startled, and wheeled out to mount his waiting pony and gallop away. That man,

Kelcy had been almost sure, was a Pitchfork cowboy.

'I'll have to move,' Sebastian said. 'That's all there is to it.'

Kelcy's eyes were worried. 'But you're in no condition to move, Clay. You've hardly been in bed two weeks. That hole in your back could still break open.'

'Better than growing another hole,' he said, and struggled up on one elbow. The pain was still there but he kept his face blank, not wanting to disturb the girl. He said: 'Saddle my horse while I put some clothes on.'

She touched his shoulder restrainingly. 'Clay . . .'

'Move,' he said, scowling. 'How long do you think it will take that rider to get to DeSpain and get back here?'

'If you're trying to make me angry, it won't work. Clay, we'll bluff him out somehow. But you've got to stay here.'

'And get killed,' he finished for her.

'No. At least wait until I can find Dan and bring him to talk to you.'

He didn't have a chance to answer; she was gone and the door was shut. Cursing mildly, he rose slowly from the bed and tested his legs. The weakness was surprising to him; the effort it took merely to stand was disturbing. Moving slowly, he crossed in bare feet to the dresser. He bent, frowning back pain, slipped on his trousers, and walked stiffly into Dan's room to

158

borrow a shirt. Then he found his socks and boots and grimaced when the weight of his gun belt settled across his hips.

All this unaccustomed activity registered on him then and he sank into the chair, just to rest for a moment.

But he was still there, his eyes half-shut, when Kelcy re-entered the room. 'Clay!'

He waved a hand in a weary gesture and struggled to his feet. Kelcy came forward with a single long stride and helped support him. She said, 'I couldn't find Dan. Clay, we can hide you in O'Keefe's storeroom until DeSpain's gone.'

He shook his head. 'It wouldn't work. DeSpain's got the bug in his head that I'm still batting around. He'll search every corner of this town. I've got to get out in the hills.'

He lurched toward the door and paused there, looking back. In the dresser mirror he saw his own reflection, gaunt and hollow-eyed; and he had to grin at himself. Kelcy said, 'I guess I can't stop you, can I?'

'No.'

'Then I'll have to ride along with you.'

'No,' he said again. 'If DeSpain caught you with me, do you think he'd show you any mercy?'

'He won't, anyway,' she said. 'He'll know I've been hiding you.'

He touched the door latch. 'You can stay with Dan. In the hills I may have to move fast.

You'd just slow me down.'

Her eyes were sad; she was watching the awkward way he moved. 'Clay, you haven't got the strength to saddle your own horse. You've got to have someone with you.'

When he thought about it he knew she was right. But he said, 'I'll manage. You go find Dan and stick close to him.'

She shook her head and pushed past him through the door. 'Wait here,' she said. 'I'll saddle two horses and bring them around.'

She was right, and he knew it; she would be safer hiding out where the last of DeSpain's wrath couldn't reach her.

When she came back he stepped outside, squinting against the sun. She dismounted and helped him into the saddle. Bulging saddlebags rested against his legs and he opened one flap, and saw the food and frying pan she had packed. He gave her a look of gratitude and said, 'All right.'

Keeping a careful watch on him, she lined her horse out beside him, and moving at a walk they aimed for the river timber. But as they were passing the last 'dobe on the fringe of town, a man came around the side of the building, stopped in his tracks, and looked up at them. The man's jaw dropped and he said, quite distinctly, 'Holy cow!' And swung toward town at a rum, flinging looks back at them over his shoulder.

Sebastian grimaced. 'Cat's out of the bag,

now. We'll have to run for it. We'll head north toward Pitchfork. Buck won't expect us to go that way.'

There was no more talk until they had passed through the timber and were out on the slowly ascending plateau that led to Pitchfork. Then Sebastian reined in and listened against the hot air. There was a horse coming back there at a hard gallop; Sebastian lifted his revolver, and turned his horse to face the back trail. 'Go on ahead,' he said; and Kelcy, wise enough to know when not to argue, rode on up the plain.

Gun up, Sebastian sat his saddle, clenching the horn with his left hand to maintain balance. The approaching horseman was making more noise now, crashing through the trees at a dead run; and then Sebastian saw him break out of the timber and continue forward without slackening pace. It took a shocking amount of energy to cock the Colt, Sebastian then allowed himself to relax slightly when he recognized the oncoming horseman: old Rob MacKenzie.

MacKenzie hauled his horse in and said gruffly, 'You can put the gun down, Clay.'

Sebastian holstered the revolver. He said, 'So now you know.'

'I kind of figured it this way all along,' the old man said. 'You're too damn tough to die, Clay, I heard in town you were riding out.'

'And?'

161

'Just thought I'd offer you my place for a hideout.'

'That's mighty thoughtful,' Sebastian observed. 'For a man who's done his best to sit the fence for a month.'

'DeSpain's gone crazier than a hydrophobia coyote,' MacKenzie said, and it was all he felt he had to say. 'Come on out to Pennant. I'll ride along with you. Maybe if Buck sees three sets of tracks together he'll figure he's on the wrong trail.'

'Obliged,' Sebastian said, and put his horse forward beside the old man. Jesse had always liked and admired MacKenzie, he remembered; but until this afternoon he had held his own tight reservations about the old man. Sebastian said, 'You may get your outfit burned out from under you.'

'I'll take the chance,' MacKenzie answered. 'You look like you need sleep.'

'Like I never needed anything,' Sebastian agreed; it was hard to keep his eyes open, hard to stay on the rocking saddle.

They caught up with Kelcy and rode in silence for two hours, straight north past the perimeter of Pitchfork, and then turned slightly northwest toward MacKenzie's high-plain ranch. Sebastian rode with his head dropped against his chest and his fists locked over the saddle horn; the world rocked and lurched and jarred him endlessly. He half-heard MacKenzie's quiet warning, 'Hold it—

hold it.'

His horse stopped and when he raised his head to look, he saw that they were stopped near the crest of a high ridge. MacKenzie was looking back toward the south; and when Sebastian looked that way he saw the long spire of dust, fanning high, that had drawn MacKenzie's attention. He heard McKenzie's long sigh. 'That'll be Pitchfork. Sooner than I expected.'

'About four miles back,' Sebastian estimated. 'You two head straight for Pennant. I'll cut into the hills and try to lose them.'

MacKenzie said, 'No. That's what he'll expect. And you're in no shape to outrun that crew, boy. Look, you and Miss Kelcy make for the ranch. I'll ride west awhile, then lose them in the rocks above Aztec Creek. They'll follow the single set of tracks, expecting it's you.'

Sebastian's head lifted. 'I can't let you do that, Rob.'

MacKenzie's voice was ugly when he said, 'You've got no choice. Now quit wasting time. I'll meet you sometime tonight at Pennant and we'll figure out how to play it from there. On the run, now.'

MacKenzie reached out to touch the rump of Sebastian's horse; the pony lurched forward and Sebastian had to concentrate on just staying aboard. When he regained his balance and looked back, he saw the fast diminishing shape of MacKenzie galloping west. Kelcy said, 'I pray he makes it.'

'He'll make it,' Sebastian lied. 'He's a wise old buzzard, and a tough one.' But inside, he wasn't as certain. He could only expect that if Pitchfork did catch MacKenzie, they would recognize him in time before they started shooting.

He paused at the top of the ridge to look back once more. To the west, MacKenzie was almost out of sight. The old man seemed deliberately to be galloping through dust pockets to make as plain a sign as he could. Sebastian shook his head. It was that kind of courage that had built this land. Southward, the advancing ball of dust grew rapidly, not more than two and a half miles away. 'Let's go,' he said, and put his horse over the top.

But they hadn't traveled ten minutes farther when he reined in, blinked a few times to clear the annoying. fog from his eyes, and said, 'This won't do.'

Kelcy said, 'What?'

But he had already put his horse off the trail to the west; and when Kelcy came up and asked questions, he did not answer.

An hour later, reeling drunkenly in the saddle, he halted the pony below a rock crest and slid out of the saddle. 'Wait here,' he said shortly to the girl, and grimly climbed the brief rise to the top. There he lay belly-down, catching his breath, and looked out over the knife-edged hills ahead.

The lonely shape of a single rider cut across a gully a scant half-mile distant and went up the far cutbank, caving in the side. MacKenzie's horse scrambled to the top and then Sebastian saw the old man pause to look back.

Behind him, not far south of Sebastian's post, the dozen men of Pitchfork drummed forward in a tightly bunched mass. DeSpain's blocky figure was in the lead. Just then someone among them spotted the fugitive ahead; and immediately the crowd broke up, splitting into two- and three-man groups to fan out over the land. Sebastian lost MacKenzie for a moment, and saw him reappear on a farther slope, heading up its length at a dead gallop. Then one of the Pitchfork riders achieved a low summit, slid out of his saddle with his rifle and took careful aim. The shot rang across the clear air, and out there on yonder slope, no more than three-quarters of a mile away, MacKenzie's horse spilled.

The dot that was MacKenzie ran farther up the slope afoot into the cover of a boulder cluster. Sebastian heard the mutter of his own bitter oaths. Across the bowl the Pitchfork men were leaving their saddles, crawling forward on foot with their rifles; and then the guns began shooting, talking across the bowl in harsh, staccato bursts. Up on the slope, occasional puffs of gunsmoke marked MacKenzie's constantly shifting position. Once

Sebastian saw DeSpain's unmistakable fat figure waddling forward through the brush. Sebastian lifted himself to his feet and palmed his revolver. It was far beyond pistol range but maybe by creating a diversion he could draw them off MacKenzie. This wasn't rightfully MacKenzie's fight.

He lifted the revolver, cocked it, and stepped forward. But then he stumbled on a loose rock and went down. When his injured side hit the rocky ground he felt the lance of terrible pain; and lost consciousness almost immediately, cursing his inability to save MacKenzie.

## CHAPTER FOURTEEN

When he looked around him he recognized once more Kelcy's bedroom. How had he gotten here? Or had he never left the room—was it all a dream?

Dan McGarrity opened the door and stepped in. Sebastian said immediately, 'How about MacKenzie?'

'He's all right,' McGarrity said. 'He surrendered to DeSpain. But it's put DeSpain in hot water now. MacKenzie's sworn out warrants against the whole crew of them for assault with a deadly weapon. I'm about to ride out to Pitchfork.'

'He'll never let you get away with it,' Sebastian said. 'How'd I get here?'

'Kelcy,' McGarrity said briefly, and it was enough. Sebastian said, 'They had MacKenzie pinned down tight when I blacked out. Thank God he made it.'

'He knows when to quit,' McGarrity said. 'Though if he'd had the chance I think he'd have gunned them all down. Take it easy, now. I'm on my way out to Pitchfork.'

Sebastian had been looking out through the window. Now he rose on one elbow and said tightly, 'You may not have to.'

McGarrity walked forward and stooped to look through the dusty pane. Sebastian heard his soft whistle. 'DeSpain, Kohlmeier, and the whole bunch.'

'Looking for me,' Sebastian said. He was already struggling out of bed. Despite last night's fall, he felt stronger this morning than he had at any time in the last two weeks. He got into his clothes and walked with stiff slowness to stand by McGarrity at the window. 'You can't cut it alone, Dan.'

'I've got a job to do,' McGarrity said and went out the door.

By this time the Pitchfork crowd had disappeared into Chaffee's. 'Council of war,' Sebastian murmured. When he saw McGarrity wasn't headed for the saloon, he allowed himself to relax. He belted on his gun and walked slowly through to the front door and opened it, and stood in its opening facing the saloon. He had known it would come to this; soon, now, DeSpain would have to come out Chaffee's door; and he had seen that DeSpain was armed today. He only hoped he had the strength to do his part.

The steady drone of voices rolled faintly from Chaffee's place. Southward, a buckboard pulled around into sight and came rocking along—the Slash-D wagon, with Fletch Diedrich on the high seat. Sebastian frowned. But Diedrich did not seem to be aware of what was transpiring in Arrowhead; he hardly seemed to give any attention to the mass of horses outside Chaffee's. He tooled the buckboard forward, pitched over a humpy section, and stopped at O'Keefe's store, where he set the brake and got down.

A quiet loneliness lay over the town. In Sebastian's nostrils mingled the odors of dust and horses and sweat-impregnated leather. Then Fletch Diedrich stumbled out of O'Keefe's, fear making his face pallid, and ran across to Chaffee's, Frowning, Sebastian watched O'Keefe's door until another figure took shape there. Then, rashly ignoring the open door of Chaffee's, Sebastian set off across the dust toward the store.

He achieved O'Keefe's porch without incident and stepped up into its shade. He said, 'What the hell are you doing here?'

'Backing your hand,' said Jeremiah Rivers,

in an idle tone. 'Maybe I can shorten the odds.'

'I told you to drift,' Sebastian said.

'You also told me I owed you a debt. I pay my debts in my own way, sir.'

Sebastian chose not to press the point. Across the wide street, Fletch Diedrich walked nervously out of Chaffee's and advanced. At Sebastian's shoulder, Jeremiah Rivers observed, 'I see he delivered my message.'

Glancing back over his shoulder, Diedrich climbed into his buckboard and lifted the reins. Rivers stepped forward into the slanted sunlight. There was a half-humorous upturn to his mouth. 'Forgot something, didn't you?'

'What?' Diedrich said.

'The supplies you came for.'

'To hell with them,' Diedrich said, and lashed the horses. The buckboard careened away, leaving its wake of dust and fear. Rivers retreated into the shade, chuckling sonorously. Just then Dan McGarrity came out of the store to stand on Sebastian's other side. 'Wonder what's keeping him so long?'

'He knows there are three of us now,' Rivers said.

Sebastian said, 'This isn't your fight.'

'I choose to make it my fight,' Rivers answered.

Sebastian nodded, not replying. Whirling through the air in streaky currents was the residual sense of Diedrich's fear, left behind to coat them all. The sun was the color of brass, making a white glare on the face of the earth.

'Standing together,' Rivers said, 'we make too easy a target.' So saying, he pushed off the porch and moved at a casual pace toward Noah Teale's blacksmith shop. He took up a post midway between that place and the livery corral, and stood with wide stance, tilting his hat against the sun, somehow managing to appear as idle as any man alive. But his eyes were bright and attentive.

O'Keefe and Kelcy came out then, and Sebastian turned toward them. 'Get back inside.'

Without argument the two turned back, Kelcy flinging him a half-sorrowful glance. But Kelcy was a girl born and bred to the harsh rules of this frontier and so she said nothing. Propped against the porch post, Sebastian heard a step and turned, about to issue another warning, when he saw it was Rob MacKenzie advancing through the door. MacKenzie said, 'I heard what you tried to do yesterday, Clay.'

'You did more for me,' Sebastian said.

MacKenzie said, 'There may be a way out of this without shootin'.'

McGarrity shook his head. 'Not with Buck DeSpain.'

'Believe I'll give it a try, anyway,' MacKenzie said in a conversational tone. He stepped off the porch and walked ten paces into the dust. 'Buck!' he called.

DeSpain took his time answering; and when he did appear he was not alone. At his left shoulder stood Lew Kohlmeier, a head taller and fifty pounds lighter. DeSpain stood just outside Chaffee's doorway. 'What you want?'

'I want to make a deal,' MacKenzie said. 'You call off your dogs and take your cows home from Hat, and I'll tear up those warrants against you and your crew.'

DeSpain's answer was immediate. 'Go to hell, Rob.'

But Lew Kohlmeier touched his elbow. 'Wait a minute, Buck. Let's talk about it.'

DeSpain's angry glance turned against Kohlmeier. But then the two men wheeled and returned to the darkness of Chaffee's. Apparently they hadn't seen McGarrity and Sebastian on the porch, though Sebastian was sure they'd seen Jeremiah Rivers slouched down by the corral.

Dan McGarrity said, 'The wrong one of those two is runnin' that show. I've got some things against Lew Kohlmeier, but I'd a lot quicker trust him for common sense than I would Buck.'

'Given half a chance,' Sebastian said, 'Lew would have been all right.' He shut his eyes for a moment, trying to summon strength. The pain in his side was dull and throbbing; his head ached and his legs felt weak.

Out in the sun, Jeremiah Rivers had stooped to pull up a yellow straw, and stuck it between his teeth. Now he, stood in an easy manner, tugging at the left side of his mustache. Rob MacKenzie came back up to the porch. 'If it was up to Kohlmeier, they'd go home. But Buck's gone loco, plumb crazy. He just don't care any more—he don't know his right hand from his left.'

As if to punctuate the statement, the hard echoes of a single gunshot crashed from Chaffee's. Instantly Dan McGarrity was surging forward; but Sebastian's restraining arm caught him and Sebastian said, 'Hold it. Don't walk into it, Dan.'

The deputy held back; and shortly thereafter a small knot of men boiled from the doorway, their backs to the street and guns in their hands. But no one fired a shot; the five men mounted their horses and wheeled away, all of them wearing shocked expressions and none of them talking. Sebastian said, 'Kohlmeier's boys. But Lew's not with them. Now, what's that mean?'

MacKenzie sighed. 'I think it means the last wire has come down in Buck's head. I think that shot was—'

Just then DeSpain's blocky shape filled the saloon doorway and MacKenzie's voice trailed off. There was a gun in DeSpain's fist and his face wore an ugly leer. He said plainly, 'Lew's dead. That's a job the law should have done long ago, McGarrity.'

'Lew never shot anybody,' McGarrity said.

172

'You're under arrest, DeSpain.'

DeSpain's roar of laughter sailed across the intervening forty yards. 'Try and make that stick, Deputy. My whole crew saw Lew draw his gun first.'

Sebastian shoved his shoulder away from the post and stood straight. With completely concealed effort, he stepped down off the porch into the sunlight. 'What do you want, Buck?'

'You,' DeSpain said. His voice was quiet. 'I want you, Clay. I want you dead.'

The remaining five Pitchfork men were fanning out behind DeSpain, now; and down the street, Sebastian heard Jeremiah Rivers' lazy talk cutting into the scene, 'Two guns right here, DeSpain. Three more on the porch there. That makes the odds about even, I'd say. Every gun on this side of the street will be lined on your belly when it starts. This the way you want it?'

DeSpain looked at Rivers, seeming to notice him for the first time. His words were automatic. 'You double-crossing back-stabber.' But for an instant reason seemed to take some hold over him.

Dust was fast settling where Kohlmeier's crew had galloped away. Sebastian felt strength draining slowly from him and he was impatient, knowing that whichever way DeSpain's unpredictable temper should turn, it would have to turn quickly, or Sebastian would be lost. DeSpain's crew was spread at five-foot intervals along the front wall of Chaffee's. Now DeSpain stepped forward two paces, the pistol hanging at arm's length, and looked from Rivers to the three men on the porch. Rivers tugged his mustache a final time and let his arm drop slowly. Sebastian stood his ground at the base of the porch, feeling the presence of MacKenzie and McGarrity behind him—and then a third presence. He heard Kelcy's voice and whirled.

Kelcy stood with a rifle crooked in her elbow. 'Go on home, Buck. You haven't a chance.'

Sebastian cursed. 'Inside, damn it—inside!'

Then Dan McGarrity moved, shoving his sister into the store, shouting, 'Stay there.' And pulled the door shut with a slam.

But their attention had been diverted for a moment and now Buck DeSpain's gun was up; centered on Sebastian's chest. DeSpain began to talk in a monotone, as though rationalizing his position to himself. 'Every way I turn there's one man in my way. That's you, Sebastian. You keep open range from me. You stampede my herds. You shoot down my men. And when one of my boys gets a crack at you, he botches it. Good God, if I had one man I could depend on . . . !'

Sebastian's stomach was sinking rapidly. As though hypnotized, he watched the steady snout of DeSpain's raised Colt. Then, down the street, he heard Rivers' voice, still unhurried, still mild, 'You've got just five seconds to drop that gun, DeSpain.'

DeSpain's bull head turned ponderously. He looked unwinkingly at Rivers. Rivers stood with that same slouched posture, his hands well away from his guns. DeSpain's lips peeled away from his teeth and it was then, in that single moment of grace, that Sebastian knew he had to move. He dived back toward the porch, uncaring of the rending pain in his body; and came to rest on the porch timbers, belly-flat, rolling over to keep his face toward DeSpain.

But DeSpain didn't even seem to notice. He was still owlishly watching Rivers. Rivers said, 'Time's almost up.' In his quiet tone rode the certainty of death.

'Damn you,' DeSpain wheezed. 'It's not you I want.' Then he whirled to face the store porch, his thumb earing back the hammer; to the last he held that single-minded purpose.

And Sebastian knew it was up to him. Lying on the porch, his gun already half-up, he knew he wasn't going to be nearly fast enough; he saw the muzzle of DeSpain's pistol coming down and then he heard two shots, so fast he could hardly distinguish them. DeSpain's body rocked and lurched but he still stood fast, like a rock, and the gun came back again into line. That was when Sebastian pulled his own trigger, and saw the bullet take off the left side of DeSpain's face.

DeSpain screamed, a high falsetto howl; and fell ponderously, burying his face in the dirt.

It was all unreal, like a half-dream. Sebastian saw Jeremiah Rivers, still standing wide-footed, but now with his two smoking, short-barreled Colts trained on the five frozen men at the saloon; and Sebastian knew then that DeSpain had dropped from the two bullets of Rivers' guns.

Dan McGarrity was crossing the street then, pausing by DeSpain's huddled body and then stepping across it, his angered talk lashing against the Pitchfork crew, 'Ride out of here and don't ever come back. Your boss is dead, and so are you if you're in Massacre Basin twenty-four hours from now.'

Jeremiah Rivers was advancing through the dust, still covering the cowboys. 'First,' Rivers said, 'you can drop your guns where you stand.'

That was all Sebastian heard. His head dropped against the planks; he felt the warm ooze of blood at his back where the half-healed wound had split open. And he shut his eyes against the sun-glare and dust and death of the day.

# CHAPTER FIFTEEN

He sat in Jesse Parrott's rocker on the porch of the sprawling Hat ranch, smoking a lazy cigarette and feeling the stiffness of his healing back and side. Out in the remuda corral, the shape of Latigo bobbed up and down on a half-broken pony. Lucio walked idly up from the barn and said, 'Hot day. I sent 'Sus out with rock salt this morning. Señor MacKenzie was at Dragoon Springs yesterday. He says to tell you the county will be auctioning off the Pitchfork steers on the first of the month.'

'Thanks, *compadre*,' Sebastian said, and watched Lucio amble back toward his never-ending work.

The sun slid over a notch and began to warm his flesh. It was good to relax, good not to worry. Ray Queene, supported on a cane, came out on the porch and settled gingerly in a chair. His face was still puffy and his left arm hung uselessly; but there was a high grin on his face and a laugh in his voice when he said, 'We're sure a pair of ugly specimens.'

Sebastian matched his grin and felt better for it. A cloud had lifted from Massacre Basin with the passing of Buck DeSpain. There would always be bleak memories but that was all. Queene said, 'Damned odd, how one man can stir up so much grief.'

'Sometimes I believe he didn't have any idea of what he was doing.'

'Yeah,' Queene said, and subsided into silence. His head turned, after a while, and he observed, 'Someone coming.'

'Let him come,' Sebastian said, with a comfortable feeling in his belly. Sunlight glinted from the blades of Lucio's newly built windmill below the tackshed. Manure and dry grass rose in the air to become a thick and heady aroma. The advancing traveler entered the yard at a trot and stepped down before the veranda, bringing a brief scowl to Sebastian's forehead. 'This is twice I thought you'd ridden on.'

'Just so,' Jeremiah Rivers said, and mounted the veranda steps. He did a strange thing then; he stood with his hat in both hands, looking down; and said, 'I've come to ask about a job.'

Sebastian shook his head. 'We don't need you, Rivers.'

'That's not what I mean,' Rivers said. 'You'll notice I'm carrying no guns.'

'Why,' Sebastian said, 'that's so.'

'I understand you're going to make a bid on those Pitchfork cattle that are up for auction.'

'Been planning on it,' Sebastian admitted.

'If you buy them, you'll need a bigger crew.'

Sebastian watched him steadily. 'You're a gun hand, Rivers. Did you ever work cattle?'

'No. But a man can learn. I'll work for food and a bed until you feel I'm worth wages.'

Sebastian regarded him, half-liking the sober evenness of Rivers' glance. 'Why are you begging for a riding job, when you can hire out at twice foreman's wages with your gun?'

Rivers shook his head. 'It's hard to explain. Maybe I just don't want to take the chance of turning out like Buck DeSpain—a man with nothing but hate and death in his soul.'

Ray Queene said softly, 'I'll buy that.'

'All right,' Sebastian said. 'Pitch your belongings in the bunkhouse and turn your horse out with the cavvy.

'My thanks,' Jeremiah Rivers murmured, and went down to lead his horse away.

'Well,' Queene said. 'What do you think of that, now?'

'I think,' Sebastian said, 'that it's a rare man who'll unbend his pride that much. I get the feeling we've just hired the makings of a top hand.'

'Believe you're right,' Queene said, and rose stiffly to journey inside the house, to Nora.

Not long thereafter the day became complete when Kelcy McGarrity came riding down the trail and joined him on the porch. Sebastian said, 'What took you so long?'

'I was helping Leila Diedrich make a dress,' she said. 'You know, I like Leila. She's the only thing that kept Fletch out of this whole rotten mess.'

'And he's a lot better off for it,' Sebastian said. For a moment his eyes displayed no

179

definite expression; then he smiled at her. A little breeze came up to sweep his warm cheeks.

Kelcy smoothed her hair and extended her hands to draw him to his feet. His steady eyes watched her, absorbing every fine detail of her features; he saw the crosswise pull of present happiness and recent tragedies in her eyes. There was the nearness of a smile, deep and warm, in back of her glance; her lips were gentle. The glow in her eyes became still and faraway, turned that way by the gravity of her thoughts. She tightened her grip on his arms, and it was in that mood—thoughtful and uncertain, yet confident of the future, that he bent his head for her kiss. She drew back and he kissed her once more, as a man kisses the woman he loves.

'That's it,' he said; 'that's all there is.'

'It's enough,' she said, and drew him to her with the pressure of her hands.